W9-BSK-055

The Queen Bee and Me

Also by Gillian McDunn

Caterpillar Summer

The
Queen Bee
and Me

Gillian McDunn

BLOOMSBURY
CHILDREN'S BOOKS
NEW YORK LONDON OXFORD NEW DELHI SYDNEY

BLOOMSBURY CHILDREN'S BOOKS
Bloomsbury Publishing Inc., part of Bloomsbury Publishing Plc
1385 Broadway, New York, NY 10018

BLOOMSBURY, BLOOMSBURY CHILDREN'S BOOKS, and the Diana logo
are trademarks of Bloomsbury Publishing Plc

First published in the United States of America in March 2020
by Bloomsbury Children's Books

Bloomsbury books may be purchased for business or promotional use.
For information on bulk purchases please contact Macmillan Corporate and
Premium Sales Department at specialmarkets@macmillan.com

Library of Congress Cataloging-in-Publication Data
Names: McDunn, Gillian, author.
Title: The queen bee and me / by Gillian McDunn.
Description: New York : Bloomsbury, 2020.
Summary: Twelve-year-old Meg is anxious about growing apart
from her best friend Beatrix, but she is also interested in learning about
the quirky new student Hazel and her backyard beehive.
Identifiers: LCCN 2019019788 (print) | LCCN 2019022392 (e-book)
ISBN 978-1-68119-751-7 (hardcover) • ISBN 978-1-68119-752-4 (e-book)
Subjects: CYAC: Best friends—Fiction. | Friendship—Fiction. | Bees—Fiction. |
Bullying—Fiction. | Middle schools—Fiction. | Schools—Fiction.
Classification: LCC PZ7.1.M43453 Qu 2020 (print) | LCC PZ7.1.M43453 (e-book) |
DDC [Fic]—dc23
LC record available at https://lccn.loc.gov/2019019788

Book design by Jeanette Levy
Typeset by Westchester Publishing Services
Printed and bound in the U.S.A. by Berryville Graphics Inc., Berryville, Virginia
2 4 6 8 10 9 7 5 3 1

All papers used by Bloomsbury Publishing Plc are natural, recyclable
products made from wood grown in well-managed forests. The manufacturing processes
conform to the environmental regulations of the country of origin.

To find out more about our authors and books visit
www.bloomsbury.com and sign up for our newsletters.

For Violet

The
Queen Bee
and Me

ANIMAL FIELDWORK PROJECT
MS. DUPART
EXPLORATORY SCIENCE
SECOND SEMESTER
SIXTH PERIOD

PART

1

Describe your subject using words and pictures. What does the animal do all day? If the animal is social, show how it contributes to keeping the society organized and running smoothly.

15 points

As a worker bee grows, so do her activities.
A young bee's first job is cleaning the honeycomb.
Then she is promoted, one job at a time.
She feeds baby bees, makes food, builds the
honeycomb, and guards the entrance to the hive.
Finally, she is old enough to go outside the hive
as a forager bee. She will fly for miles to collect
nectar, pollen, and water.

How does the worker bee realize it is time
to switch to something new? No one knows. The
important thing is that the bee herself knows
when it is time for a change.

CHAPTER 1

There are two kinds of people in the world: those who want to look inside to see how stuff works and those who couldn't care less.

I've always been the first kind of person.

My earliest memory is from when I was three years old, sitting on top of the kitchen table and taking apart our toaster. I was a nervous little kid, and somehow Mom figured out that learning about the insides of things would calm me. She says I have a jumpy kind of brain and need something to put that energy into, which is how she was as a kid, too.

So one day, she plopped me on the table and looked at me seriously.

"These are the rules, Meg," she said. "You have to ask first. You can never touch anything that is still plugged in. And most important: if you take it apart, you have to put it together again."

Then she placed the toaster on the table between us. She showed me how to use the screwdriver to loosen and tighten. She showed me that, sometimes, pieces need a little wiggle before they slide open. When the insides are revealed, all the mysteries are solved. Each piece has its place. Everything fits just right.

That morning in the kitchen, Mom explained the coiled springs and balanced levers. She showed me the wires that radiate heat to toast the bread. And after I was done looking, Mom let me put it back together again.

Since then, I've taken apart clocks, radios, blenders, and once a microwave. When the world feels confusing, it helps to look at the pieces and see how they fit.

Putting them back together is harder. I do my best, but when springs uncoil and levers unbalance, it changes things. They're as good as new—almost.

When I was little, I thought that if I looked hard enough, I could understand the whole world that way. But lately, I'm not so sure that's right. Some things can't handle being cracked open. If I look too closely, some things might make *less* sense. Or they may fall apart completely.

"Hel-*lo?*" says Beatrix, interrupting my thoughts. Beatrix is my best friend, but right now she doesn't look very friendly.

Oops. I look at her blankly. My thoughts pinwheel backward, trying to remember the moment just before I stopped paying attention.

"Earth to Meg?" Beatrix crosses her arms tightly, like she's giving herself an angry hug. "Are you even listening?"

I *wasn't*, but I can't say that.

Here's something else I can't say:

Beatrix Bailey is my best friend. I love her, but I don't always like her.

The thought is sharp, like it's made of broken glass. But it feels like the truth. Maybe that's why it hurts so much.

CHAPTER

2

She stands still and looks at me, frowning. She's waiting for me to answer.

My tangle of thoughts had me in outer space. Now I'm zoomed all the way back to Earth, to North Carolina, to the Willow Pond Middle School soccer field, where we do slow laps with Bart and Lola every Tuesday, rain or shine. They're the last clients left from our fourth-grade dog-walking business, the one that was supposed to make us rich by middle school.

"Sorry," I say. I wonder how much of the conversation I missed.

Beatrix's eyes are light blue, the color of a swimming

pool. Right now they are narrowed in a frown. "Seriously? You weren't paying attention?"

"Um," I say. If I tell her the truth, she will be furious.

Beatrix rewraps her scarf against the January chill. I rub my hands against my cheeks, trying to warm them. Without even looking into a mirror, I can tell my face is red. My usually pale skin turns into a shade of lobster whenever it gets windy like this. Meanwhile, Beatrix's skin is golden from her family's recent tropical vacation— never chapped or rashy.

Lola, at her feet, sniffs the straw-colored grass, barely noticing when Bart flops into a sit beside her, panting. He gives me a slobbery smile, like he's proud of what a good dog he is.

Then I figure out what to say.

"Dance," I say. "You were talking about dance." This is a safe guess. For Beatrix, dancing is life—she's always leaping and twirling randomly throughout the day to get her point across.

Beatrix starts walking again, and I hurry to follow.

"*Anyway*," she says. "I was talking about the spring recital. For our dance elective? I don't want a repeat of what happened last week."

"Me neither," I say, thinking of how I stumbled through the performance—two hours of my life I'll never get back.

"I hate getting lost in those giant group dances," says

Beatrix. "They're so awkward, and the audience can't even see who's doing what."

"Um, Beatrix?" I say. "Getting lost in those big group dances is the only way I survive those dance recitals!"

She laughs like I'm joking, but I'm not. When I dance, it's like my brain and my body are speaking different languages. The only reason I've suffered through the last three semesters of dance is because of her. Last year, I tried to switch to art. But when I told her my plan, she got furious. Then she froze me out. She didn't speak to me for an entire week. I hated that feeling even more than I hate dance.

"I mean it," I say. "I'm not like you. I'm the worst one in the class."

Beatrix shakes her head. "You would be better if you worked harder. Then you would like it more."

I'm pretty sure I've heard Mrs. Bailey say that exact same thing to Beatrix before. I doubt she realizes it.

"Maybe," I say. I reach into my pocket and feel the folded piece of paper. There's something I need to tell Beatrix. Maybe I should just do it now.

But when I think of last year and The Freeze, I stop myself. I may not always like her, but I don't want to lose her, either.

"Why are you worried about dance elective anyway?" I ask. "It's months away, and it's not anything like the fancy recitals you do for ballet."

Beatrix pulls Lola's leash to keep her on the path. "My

'fancy' ballet studio isn't all that great," she says. She uses her fingers to make air quotes when she says *fancy*.

I shrug. "It's a whole lot better than the Willow Pond Middle auditorium," I say. For some reason, the auditorium always smells like feet.

Beatrix sniffs. "They wouldn't even give me the part I wanted for *Nutcracker.* I've been working for years to be Clara, and now I'm suddenly too tall. I had to be a Russian dancer, which was ridiculous."

I frown. I knew Beatrix was disappointed when she didn't get Clara, but when it happened she acted like it didn't bother her. She said being a Russian dancer was technically difficult, maybe more challenging than Clara. But I guess that wasn't really the truth.

"No way," I say. "You were so good as a Russian dancer. That part looked really hard, and you nailed it."

Beatrix smiles slightly, then shakes her head like she's erasing it. "Nothing is as good as a solo. If I get stuck doing group dances, we'll never make it to New York."

I lift my hand to my mouth and bite the skin next to my thumb, my nervous habit that won't go away. "Oh, right. New York."

Beatrix is going to be a ballerina in New York someday, just like her mom was. Beatrix has it all planned: after high school, we'll live there together. Even though cities make me nervous. Even though I like it fine right here in Willow Pond.

Beatrix tilts her head to the side. "Besides, at least elective is mostly contemporary. Ballet is so *ugh* sometimes, you know? Even though I know I'm excellent at it." She pauses and looks at me. "Not to brag."

She waits for me to agree. It is a half-brag, even if it's true—but I nod anyway.

"But when I do contemporary, I don't think about getting the best part, or who's watching me," she says. "I feel like I'm completely and totally myself."

Science. That's how I feel when I'm learning about science. The thought is in my head so fast, it's almost like the speed of light. Maybe I should tell her the truth. I'm doing the science elective Ms. Dupart recommended me for, the one seventh graders take only by special invitation.

I'm about to say the words, and then I see her face.

"You're the only one who understands me," she says. An inky strand of hair has come loose from her perfect ponytail and is stuck to her cheek. "Thanks. I mean it."

So I close my mouth. I chicken out. I'm the only one who understands Beatrix. And I don't want to make her mad. When she gave me The Freeze last year, it was the worst week of sixth grade. We've been best friends since kindergarten, and I don't want that to change. I don't want her to be mad at me, or sad at me, or whatever would make her stop talking to me again.

So instead I nod. "Yeah. Of course."

Beatrix smiles. It's a nice moment, one we haven't had

for a while. It reminds me of the old days of Beatrix-and-Meg, when everyone called us that—even our parents—like it was all one name together. Back then, the line where Beatrix ended and I began was softer, blurred somehow. It had seemed that best friends didn't need to be separate.

"The sun's going down," she says. "Let's run the rest of the way home."

Before I can answer, she takes off. Lola bounds beside her.

My hands are cold and stinging, so I hurry to catch up. Bart's ears flop as he runs alongside me.

She doesn't turn her head to see if I'm coming. She knows I will always follow.

CHAPTER

3

We run without stopping all the way to the Fletchers'
house. The wind blows harder, and it feels like needles on
my face. We return Bart and Lola to Mrs. Fletcher, and
then we walk to the halfway point between our houses,
where our streets intersect.

It's funny how two streets in the same neighborhood
can feel so different. My street, Sycamore Avenue, is a
regular street. The houses aren't the biggest and aren't the
smallest—it's somewhere in between. Poplar Terrace has
the fancy houses, and Beatrix's, at the top of the hill, is the
fanciest of all.

"Why does winter have to be so cold?" Beatrix groans.

I stamp my feet, trying to warm them. "After dinner, do you want to do homework together?"

Beatrix rubs at a muscle in her neck. "Can't. I don't have dance tonight, but we're getting ready for Sunday."

The Baileys have parties every few months, and everyone in the neighborhood is invited. Sometimes it seems like the whole town is there. I used to think the parties were all about the Baileys being friendly, but Beatrix says it's so her mom can keep up her real estate contacts. Maybe it's both.

"But that's five whole days away," I say.

Beatrix's face tightens. "You know how it is. Everything has to be perfect."

Their house always looks straight out of a catalog anyway, but for parties it somehow looks even perfect-er.

I touch my face. "My nose is officially numb."

"All right," she says. "I better go."

"Toodle-oo, caribou," I say. It's an inside joke, what Mrs. Zimmerman would say at the end of the day when we were in kindergarten.

"Take care, polar bear," Beatrix says automatically, but then she squinches her eyes shut, like she tasted something sour.

"What's wrong?" I ask.

Beatrix frowns. "Meg, we have to stop doing animal goodbyes. It's too babyish."

Heat creeps into my frozen cheeks. "It's just a joke."

"We're halfway through seventh grade. We have to be more mature." She says it like it's all settled.

I jam my hands deep in my pockets and watch her walk away, ponytail swinging. We aren't babies anymore—I know that. But saying goodbye that way has always been our thing. Maybe Beatrix feels grown up all the time, but I sure don't. Sometimes I still feel like a kid on the inside. I thought she did, too.

On the way home, I don't rush, even though it's so cold that my breath turns to clouds. When I get to my house, I somehow feel warmer just looking at it. It's not that the house is anything all that special. It looks like the kind of house little kids draw—a square with a triangle roof. It's the inside that makes it special. I push open the front door, and the smell of Dad's roasted chicken hits me. There's nothing better in the world.

Dad and Conrad are in the kitchen, listening to the news podcast Mom and I can't stand, the one that feels like yelling. But it's not turned on too loud, and they both seem to be in a great mood. Conrad is fifteen. He grew a lot last summer but hasn't gained weight yet. He's so skinny, he has sharp corners everywhere. Mom says he's all elbows and knees.

"Hey," Dad says when he sees me. He's mashing potatoes with extra garlic, just how I like them. "Can you set the table? Mom is picking up Elsie from Grandma Lou's."

Elsie is two years old. People like to comment on the

14

ten-year gap between Elsie and me, but my parents just smile and say she's the best surprise they ever got.

Conrad frowns at the cucumber he is supposed to be chopping. "Am I supposed to take the seeds out? I can never remember."

My family got serious about family meals when Conrad joined the high school marching band. When he started missing dinners, Mom put her foot down. She says he can't spend more time with his tuba than he does with the family. So now we have family dinner at least once a week. Instead of sitting at the kitchen counter or randomly grabbing something to eat, the five of us sit at the dining table together. We even use cloth napkins. Conrad and I roll our eyes about it a little, but I think we both like it. Besides, Elsie knows how to keep things interesting.

I hear Mom's car, and then Elsie bursts through the door. She's wearing purple plastic princess shoes. I'm guessing they're a gift from Grandma Lou, who picks up Elsie three afternoons a week so they can spend time together, like she did when Conrad and I were little. Grandma Lou wears interesting necklaces and always smells of perfume. Elsie thinks Grandma Lou is fabulous.

"Hi! Hi! Hi!" Elsie stomps down the hall, swinging a yellow purse. Her shoes go *clackety-clack*.

"Hey, Elsie," I say. "Did Grandma pick you up from school? What did you do?"

Instead of answering, she turns over her purse and

shakes it until three plastic tigers fall out. The littlest one is always called Elsie. She calls the other two "Mom and Dad" or "Meg and Conrad," depending on her mood.

"My messy tigers!" She holds them up. They're covered with white powder.

"Uh-oh," I say, leaning down to see. "How did they get messy?"

"I fed them a doughnut," Elsie says. "I fed them *two* doughnuts. *One. Two!*"

She presses the tigers against her cheeks and then races down the hall to Dad.

Elsie might be everyone's favorite. She's adorable, and not just in that "all little kids are cute" kind of way. The rest of us look pretty much the same. We all have fair skin, brownish hair, and grayish eyes. Elsie has bright-red hair, ocean-blue eyes, and deep dimples. Grandma Lou calls her skin "peaches and cream." I don't know about that, but I do know that someday I want to know enough genetics to understand why Elsie looks so different from the rest of us.

Soon Mom is inside, kicking her work shoes into the basket by the door. She works as an engineer for a dental supply company. She helped design the machine that packages the flavored stuff dentist offices use to clean teeth. When she was busy building it, she brought home sample flavors for us to try. We all agreed that Razzleberry was best, but Coconut Dream was just plain disgusting.

"Dinner smells heavenly." She goes over and kisses Dad and then gives quick hugs to Conrad and me.

I help carry plates to the table. Elsie refuses to sit in her booster seat, even though she's too short for a regular chair. She barely peeks over the edge of the table as Mom arranges chicken chunks, mashed potatoes, and green beans directly on the Binky Bunnies place mat. Elsie's not big on eating, so most of this is for show.

"How was school today?" Dad asks after we all sit down. "The last week of the semester, right?"

While Conrad complains about his math exam, I scoot the potatoes around on my plate. All I can think of is that folded paper in my pocket.

"What about you, Meg?" Mom turns to me, but Elsie interrupts.

"Today I did clay at school. See?" She picks up two small handfuls of potatoes and smashes them together. Then she grabs another scoop and does it again. Conrad snickers.

Mom frowns slightly. A few strands of hair have escaped her bun, and I notice that she's getting more gray. She hasn't had time to do her highlights lately. "Elsie, not with your food."

"I'm squishing it!" Elsie says proudly.

Mom sighs, reaching over to wipe Elsie's hands. "No squishing with food. Only with clay."

Dad grins and shakes his head. "Any big tests for you, Meg?"

"I have a little homework tonight—nothing huge." I clear my throat. "And I need a parent signature on something."

Mom looks at me, questioningly.

I take the paper from my pocket. "It's a permission form for the advanced science elective."

Dad beams. I can't help smiling.

"Meg, that's wonderful!" Mom says.

Conrad raises his eyebrows. "Advanced science elective is for eighth graders, but you're only in seventh."

Sometimes he acts like he's the boss of Willow Pond Middle because he went there before I did.

"This year they're offering spots to four seventh graders," I say. "I'm one of them."

Conrad swallows a huge bite and wipes his mouth. "Don't do it. Electives should be fun and easy—not another class where you have to work for a grade."

"Working for a grade is a good thing," Dad says pointedly. Conrad's grades took a dip this year, and my parents definitely noticed.

"You should be an office helper," Conrad says, helping himself to another serving of potatoes. "That was the easiest class."

I shake my head. "I love science, and Ms. Dupart is great. I just don't know how to tell Beatrix."

Mom looks confused, which makes my insides twist with guilt. I never told my family about Beatrix freezing me out. How can I explain it to them when I don't understand it myself? Beatrix and I are all mixed up in each other's lives. We've been best friends for so long, we're locked in orbit—like the Earth and Moon. Nothing is ever going to change that.

"She'll be happy for you, won't she? It's such an honor to be asked," Dad says.

I shrug. "I guess. She might be sad I won't be in dance anymore." The kind of sad where she might stop talking to me.

"*Bee-twix!*" Elsie shouts, making everyone jump in their seats. "I like Bee-twix," Elsie continues. "Her is so fancy."

Dad frowns. "Friends take different classes all the time. I can't imagine it would be a big deal."

"Spoken like someone who's never been a twelve-year-old girl," Mom says. She eats a bite of salad and chews thoughtfully.

I look up. Maybe I *could* tell Mom about what's going on with Beatrix. She was once a kid. She might understand after all.

But then she continues. "For middle school girls, friends are everything. When I moved halfway through middle school, I was devastated. Not having a place to sit at lunch is the worst thing possible for a seventh-grade girl."

Mom thinks middle school is terrible, but according to her, it's because she moved so much growing up. She doesn't understand how someone who has lived in the same place her whole life could have any problems with friends.

I make a perfect forkful with chicken, potato, and a single green bean, then eat it all in one bite. I wish I could change the subject.

"Bee-twix, Bee-twix, Bee-twix," Elsie chants as she shoves green beans under her place mat.

Mom sighs. "Meg is one of the lucky ones. I always say, all you need is one good friend. I wish I'd had that in middle school."

Dad pats Mom's hand. "I would have been your friend." He says it in a jokey way, but they give each other mushy smiles.

Conrad rolls his eyes dramatically. "We get it. You guys like each other." He stands up and begins clearing the table.

Mom touches my arm. "Is that all that's bothering you?"

Ever since I got the letter inviting me to the class, a knot has been forming in my stomach. If I told her about Beatrix, I'd have to explain all the way back to The Freeze last year. It feels too big to talk about. Without thinking, I sneak my thumb up to my mouth so I can chew on the skin there.

Mom catches my hand in midair. "Just talk to Beatrix. She's your friend and wants you to be happy. You can't let your anxiety get the best of you."

I sigh. Mom always thinks it's my anxiety. When I was little, it was strong. So many things scared me: flying insects, toilets that flushed automatically, men who had mustaches. I cried easily and even fainted a few times. My doctor said it was from being so nervous my body couldn't take it anymore. Mom is still looking at me.

"Okay," I say finally. "I'll talk to her."

Mom smiles. I feel a pang. I can tell she thinks she solved the problem. I wish it were that easy.

Meanwhile, Elsie climbs down from her chair. She runs off, shrieking, aiming for the couch. Mom chases after her, trying to catch her before she wipes her messy hands. Elsie is quick, but Mom is quicker. She captures Elsie and swings her up in a hug. Over Mom's shoulder, Elsie waves at me as Mom carries her upstairs for a bath.

Loading the dishwasher, I think about Mom's words. I know Mom thinks I'm afraid to tell Beatrix about the science elective, and I guess she's right. But it's not true that this feeling is the same as the anxiety I had when I was little. When I was little, most of the things I was afraid of couldn't really hurt me. The difference now is that I know Beatrix could.

CHAPTER

4

Maybe one of Albert Einstein's theories could explain why time passed faster than usual this week. Somehow, here it is on Sunday afternoon, and I still haven't found a way to tell Beatrix about the science elective.

I kept looking for the perfect time, when it was just the two of us. But in morning carpool, a parent drives us. At lunch, we sit with Zoe and Arshi. After school, Beatrix rushes off to ballet. Plus, this week she spent all her spare time helping her mom for the party.

But I know that if I really wanted to talk to her, I could have found the time. The truth is I'm too afraid of what she might say. And even more afraid of what she might do.

Someday, The Freeze could last longer than a week. Someday Beatrix might freeze me out forever. The idea makes my stomach do a flip.

I sit at the kitchen counter, watching Mom check on her famous meatballs. She made a double batch for the Baileys' party this afternoon. I can smell them as they cook, bubbling away in a sauce made from grape jelly and Mom's secret ingredients.

She hands me a spoon. "Taste-test for me? Careful— it's hot."

I blow on it until it's cool enough to eat. When I take a bite, my mouth fills with a sweet-and-spicy flavor. I smile, giving Mom a thumbs-up. Grape jelly meatballs may sound weird, but they are my absolute favorite.

Conrad, upstairs, crashes on his drums. He's played the tuba for years, but at Christmas, he begged for a drum set so he can "experiment musically." Mostly this means playing along with classic rock songs, using extra cymbals. I've heard that song "Tom Sawyer" about a thousand times since December, and I still have no idea what it is about. Even worse, sometimes Conrad pauses it when he needs to do an extra-long drum solo. I don't know if my ears will ever be the same.

Mom must be thinking the same thing. She gazes at the ceiling, shaking her head. "I can't believe Elsie is sleeping through that."

I grin at her. "Lucky Elsie."

She laughs and then covers her mouth quickly, as if she could put it back in.

"Oh, *Meg*," she says, in a half-scolding way. She's always so serious about supporting us with our interests, but the truth is that Conrad should stick to the tuba.

"Oh, *Mom*," I say back, and she laughs. "But seriously, you should be glad she's napping."

"Good point," says Mom. "A two-year-old without a nap is a challenge on a regular day, not to mention on a party day."

Before Elsie was born, I didn't really get the point of babies. But once I looked into her scrunched-up newborn face and touched her fuzzy hair, I decided she was okay. Now it's hard to imagine our family without her.

Mom looks at the clock and sighs. "I need to pack these up for the party and take them to the Baileys. Then I'll run back here, wake Elsie, and make sure Dad and Conrad are showered and presentable."

Dad's job is designing board games. He works from home, and Mom says that's why he doesn't notice that his clothes tend to have holes or be worn thin. But I think Dad would dress like that even if he worked in an office. He says clothes are more comfortable when they've been lived in a bit.

She wipes at a glob of applesauce crusting her sleeve. "And find time to get myself ready, come to think of it."

I can't help but notice that she looks tired.

"Mom," I say. "Why don't I take the meatballs to the Baileys' house? That way you won't feel rushed."

The minute the words are out, I realize that it's perfect. If I get to the party early, I can tell Beatrix right away, before everyone gets there. She can't get too mad with a houseful of chatting adults and about a hundred kids playing Ping-Pong in the basement. We'll spend the rest of the afternoon hanging out together, like we always do.

Mom looks skeptical. "It's a double batch, so they're heavy. About twelve pounds, I think."

I shrug. "That's nothing. And besides, it's not far to Beatrix's."

Mom reaches out and touches my hair. "I appreciate it. Thank you."

She digs in the cabinet for two extra-big containers, transfers the meatballs, and clicks the lids on top. Then she rummages in a different cupboard. "Where are my reusable bags?"

She can't find one, so she puts them in a paper bag from the grocery store. I lift the bag, which is heavier than I thought it would be. But I can do it.

"Thanks again," Mom says. "Have fun with Beatrix." She heads for the stairs, probably hurrying to get ready while Elsie naps.

I put on my coat, then lug the meatballs through the kitchen door and into the wintry afternoon.

After I walk for about a minute, I start to think about

neutron stars, which are what's left after a star explodes. Supposedly, they are one of the densest forms of matter. But I'm starting to think that maybe scientists should study Mom's meatballs, because my fingers are about to break off.

I sidestep a patch of snow that hasn't thawed from a recent storm. Willow Pond doesn't get much snow, and what comes usually melts quickly. But on shady parts of the street, a patch of snow or ice can last for days. I don't cut the corner across Mr. Shaw's yard when I turn onto Poplar. Mr. Shaw has thick, white hair and mean eyes. He is our neighborhood grump. One time, when I was four, I picked one of his flowers. He yelled so much that I learned my lesson right then and there. I avoid him because it's not worth making him mad. Honestly, I'm still a little afraid of him. I'm used to that.

What I'm not used to is being afraid of Beatrix.

I hate feeling this way about my best friend, but it wasn't always like this. After middle school started, something changed. When we were little, I thought she was powerful—almost magic. On the first day of kindergarten, I was crying quietly in the sandbox. A boy had taken my shovel. Beatrix stomped over, braids swinging. She scowled at him until he dropped it, but we didn't stay to dig.

"Sandboxes are for babies anyway," she said. "Let's play mermaids."

That was the day we became best friends. Beatrix

introduced me to a world of unicorns and drop-off play-dates and pancakes with whipped cream. I never went back to the sandbox again. And if sometimes I missed the feeling of sand between my fingers, the feeling of a heavy scoop against my shovel, it didn't matter. I had something better. I had Beatrix.

The memory of how we became friends has always made me feel warm and safe. But now I wonder what would have happened if she hadn't rescued me. I'm sure I would have stopped crying eventually. Probably, I would have found my own shovel. Then Beatrix might be best friends with someone else. If I hadn't followed Beatrix out of the sandbox that day, maybe everything would be different.

My thoughts twist as I trudge up the hill. My fingers are stiff and cold.

I hurry into the driveway. All I can think about is getting inside so my hands can thaw.

I don't see the girl standing in my way. I bump smack into her.

And drop twelve pounds of grape jelly meatballs on Beatrix Bailey's driveway.

CHAPTER 5

The meatballs crash to the ground with a *thud*.

"I'm sorry! I didn't see you!" says the girl.

I stand there for a moment, still. I'm afraid to find out if the meatballs are wrecked. And also, I'm looking at the girl. The first thing I notice is her skin, which is somehow paler than mine. But hers is splotched with fire-engine-red patches of acne. Her entire face must hurt. It's worse than any breakout I've ever seen.

The second thing I notice is her hat. Lumpy and knitted with thick stitches, it looks like a pumpkin. Leaves perch alongside a thick stem. I've never seen this kid before in my life. She's memorable, that's for sure.

But when the girl smiles, it happens like a supernova,

bright and shining. Her smile is so kind and friendly. It almost makes me forget about her skin and weird hat.

"Sorry I bumped you," I say. "Are you okay?"

"I'm fine," she says. "Are you?"

I nod. I look at the driveway. The bag is torn, but I don't see any leaking. That has to be a good sign.

She picks up a container. "Whoa, this is heavy. What's in there?"

"Meatballs," I answer. "If they didn't break."

The girl grins, balancing the container in her arms. "I don't think the driveway could break the meatballs. But maybe these meatballs could break the driveway."

This makes me giggle. She seems nice, even though I almost knocked her over. She wears an oversized sweater with a bunch of skinny scarves draped around her neck. Her leggings are tucked into knee-high socks with bold yellow and black stripes.

Most girls at Willow Pond Middle dress the same, like an unofficial uniform. Wearing the right brand is important. People care about clothes. It's strange to see someone my age wearing something so different.

As I look at her outfit, I realize that she took some time putting it together. It's not the outfit of a person who doesn't care. It's the outfit of a person who cares about different things.

"I'm Meg," I say.

"Hazel," she says, her grin somehow widening. "I just moved in, on Maple Way."

That explains why I don't recognize her.

"Do you live in Mrs. Johnston's house?" Beatrix and I used to walk Mrs. Johnston's miniature poodle, Gloria. Mrs. Johnston always made oatmeal cookies for us on days we came by.

Hazel nods. "It's huge compared to our apartment in Newford."

I look at her out of the corner of my eye. Newford is a big city about an hour away. I've been there, but I've never heard of anyone from there moving here. Most people from the big city aren't interested in small towns.

I realize she's still holding the meatballs. "Here, I can take that."

I reach for the container, but Hazel shakes her head.

"I'll help carry them," she says.

"Okay." My fingers feel frozen, but I pick up the other container. With two of us carrying them, hopefully they won't drop again.

We walk together up Beatrix's winding driveway.

Hazel shifts the container from one arm to the other. "My mom wanted a change. Our rent kept going up, for one. And she felt like the schools would be better somewhere else. When her company had a position out here, she said yes. Before I knew it, we were moving."

She shrugs like it's not a big deal, but her voice shakes a little.

"What grade are you in?" I ask instead.

"I'm in seventh, and I start tomorrow. The only class I know is science elective," she says.

"Me too!" I blurt out the words.

She beams at me. "Really? That's so cool. I'm glad I'll know someone!"

I nod. "You'll love the teacher." I smile when I think of Ms. Dupart and her colorful clothes. I think she might enjoy Hazel's personal style.

"Whoa," says Hazel as we get closer to Beatrix's house. "This place is gigantic."

"Yeah," I say. The Bailey house is about three times bigger than mine, plus it has a media room in the attic and a giant finished basement. From the top of the hill, we can see past Beach Lake, almost all the way to Newford.

"X factor," Hazel reads the little flag that hangs by the side of the driveway. "What does that mean?"

"So everyone has an 'X' in their names," I explain. "Beatrix, she's the youngest, is in seventh grade, too. Her brothers are Dexter, Maxwell, and Knox, who is in college this year. They're all two years apart. And Mrs. Bailey's first name is Alex. It's kind of their thing."

Hazel seems to think it over. "And the dad? He must be Xavier. Or Xerxes?"

"Well, his name is Robert. His name doesn't match. But other than that, it works."

She nods, but I can't tell what she thinks.

We are almost at the house. The Baileys' dogs bark to

announce our arrival. They raise Boston Terriers, who are clownish and adorable. They like to make a fuss whenever someone comes up the path.

We head for the side door. Inside, the kitchen is a whirl-wind, with platters clattering, glasses clinking, and catering staff everywhere. Soft music is playing in the background.

"Whoa," Hazel says again, under her breath this time.

Mrs. Bailey spots us and crosses our way. Her hair, which is the same shade as Beatrix's, is slicked back in a low ponytail. She limps slightly, which is from an old ballet injury. Rocco, my favorite of Beatrix's dogs, trots behind her. He's always on the lookout for a random scrap of food, especially if that food happens to be string cheese or salami.

When Mrs. Bailey reaches us, she smiles, but it's a mouth-only smile. It doesn't show in her eyes. I know she's Beatrix's mom and all, but I try to avoid her on party days. She gets stressed out.

"Ah," she says. "Your mom's grape jelly meatballs."

I pause for a moment. There's something in her voice that sounds strange. But then she smiles brightly.

"Can't have a party without them, can we?" she says.

Hazel and I stand there awkwardly, still holding the meatballs. Mrs. Bailey narrows her eyes and looks at Hazel, like she is taking in the whole picture and isn't thrilled about what she sees. Her gaze lingers on Hazel's face, bumpy with acne, then moves to her multicolored scarves and striped socks. Hazel removes the pumpkin hat and tucks it under her arm. Her hair underneath is short, blond, and wispy, like cotton candy.

"I don't think we've met," Mrs. Bailey says finally. "I'm Beatrix's mom."

"I'm Hazel. We just moved in a few blocks over."

"The sweet little cottage on Maple? Two bed, one bath with a big, sunny yard?" Mrs. Bailey asks. As a real estate agent, she seems to know everything about our town. "Mrs. Johnston mentioned she found renters."

"Yeah." Hazel hesitates, then corrects herself. "I mean, yes, ma'am."

"You'll have to stay for the party, then," Mrs. Bailey says. "You're part of our neighborhood now."

Hazel hesitates. "I don't want to intrude."

Mrs. Bailey waves her arms at the busy kitchen around her. "Don't be silly. You'll get to meet some of the other kids. Goodness knows, we'll have a full house. Not quite sure how it happens."

It's not exactly true that Mrs. Bailey doesn't know how it happens. She sends postcards, texts, and reminders through email. The Baileys love to host these giant parties.

"You'll have to excuse me—there's so much to do," says Mrs. Bailey. "But Beatrix is in her room. Meg knows the way. Meatballs on the back counter, please."

She walks away, calling for Dexter to take Rocco down to the basement with Valentine and the other dogs, like he was supposed to do an hour ago.

We find a spot for the meatballs on the counter.

"Beatrix's room is upstairs," I say, pointing to the back staircase.

Hazel bites her lip. "I don't even know them. Are you sure it's okay that I'm at their party?"

My stomach twists when I remember the way Mrs. Bailey looked at Hazel like she didn't belong. But the Baileys invite everyone who lives in Willow Pond, so now that includes Hazel, too. "It will be fine," I say, and hope I'm right.

I head for the stairs, and Hazel follows. She walks slowly, examining the family pictures that line the stairwell in matching frames. I hardly notice those photos anymore. But Hazel pauses at each one, like she's in a museum.

"It's like they're from a magazine," she says. "They're perfect."

I know exactly what Hazel means. The Baileys are one of those families where all the boys look the same—blond hair and tall, like Mr. Bailey. And Beatrix and her mom match, too, with black hair and pale blue eyes. They are all white, just like me, but they never get sunburned like I do. Beatrix says it's because they're part French-Canadian, but I think maybe she made that up.

I pause and look at one of Beatrix by herself when she was probably in fourth grade, standing gracefully in a ballet pose. She has always been the kind of kid people notice. Not because she is the prettiest (although she is pretty) or the smartest (although she is smart). She may not even be the most talented, although I would never say that to her, especially where dance is concerned. She has something extra—a brightness, a shininess—that makes people like her. And it makes people want to *be* like her, too.

Hazel stops in front of a picture of the Baileys on Gingerbread Island, where they have a second house as big and fancy as this one. Hazel's hand is extended in midair in front of it, like she managed to stop herself just before she touched the glass.

I want to tell her that my family doesn't have pictures like this, either. In our pictures, Mom always squints, Dad is constantly rumpled, and Conrad's smile is goofy. We can barely get Elsie to sit still for ten seconds before she starts demanding to *see* the picture on the camera—the picture that hasn't been taken yet. My family doesn't wear coordinated sweaters. We don't have a giant beach house on a beautiful island.

But the Baileys have all those things, and when I look at this picture, it is easy to believe that they are absolutely perfect. Everyone wearing sweaters, all the boys with wide grins, Beatrix and her mom with smooth, shiny hair, even in the ocean breeze.

We're so busy looking at the pictures that I don't hear the footsteps on the landing.

"Hey," says Beatrix. "What are you doing?"

I stand up quickly. My stomach prickles like I've been doing something wrong. By the look on Beatrix's face, maybe I have been.

CHAPTER

6

All my muscles tense, but I try not to show it.

"Oh, hey," I say, making my voice light. "We were coming to find you."

Beatrix turns to Hazel and studies her. "Who are you? Are you friends with one of my brothers?"

Out in the driveway, Hazel didn't seem especially upset when I dropped meatballs at her feet. She did okay with Mrs. Bailey, whose glossy perfection could throw off anyone. But under Beatrix's gaze, she looks unsteady.

Hazel recovers quickly. "I'm Hazel—I just moved here from Newford. Your mom said I should come up?"

"I bumped into her outside," I say. *"Literally."*

Hazel laughs. Beatrix's eyes dart back and forth between us. I can tell she's trying to figure something out.

"Hazel's in seventh grade, too," I add.

"Oh," says Beatrix. "You're big for seventh grade."

"Big" is one of those words that doesn't always sound nice.

Hazel's grin fades a bit. *"Tall."*

"What?" asks Beatrix.

"Never mind," mumbles Hazel. She looks like she's starting to think that being in Beatrix Bailey's house is not a good idea. My ears feel warm. It's my fault that this is happening. Hazel wouldn't be here if it wasn't for me. I should find a way to smooth things over.

"She starts school tomorrow," I say.

"Tell us your schedule," Beatrix says. "We can tell you about the teachers and if you have anyone good in your classes."

Hazel shifts on the step. "I don't have my schedule yet."

"Oh," says Beatrix. She sounds disappointed.

Hazel brightens. "I know I'm in science elective, though."

Hazel glances at me, and in an instant, I know exactly what she's going to say. There's no way to stop it.

"You know," she says, "same as Meg."

Oh no.

Beatrix narrows her eyes. "Meg isn't taking science elective. She's taking dance." She looks at me, expecting me to agree.

My throat squeezes, and I can't say the words. I shake my head slowly.

Beatrix's eyes widen, and she sucks in her breath sharply. I don't know if she's more surprised or hurt.

"Right. I forgot you already told me that," she says smoothly. "I knew of course. After all, Meg *is* my best friend."

I force a smile like everything is fine, but I feel like kicking myself. I really messed up by not telling her sooner.

A voice from the kitchen floats upstairs. "Hazel? Are you up there?"

"Oops," says Hazel. "Sounds like my mom came looking for me. I better go talk to her."

Beatrix and I watch as Hazel makes her way downstairs, weaving through the kitchen as she follows her mom's voice.

"That. Was. Weird." Beatrix says each word like it's an entire sentence.

"Which part?" I ask.

"The whole thing," she snaps. "Why didn't you tell me you were taking science elective?"

My mind spins. I can't come up with a good answer, so I settle on the truth.

"I thought you'd be mad," I say.

Beatrix's eyes are narrowed. "When were you going to tell me? Or was I supposed to find out tomorrow, when you didn't show up at dance?"

"I was going to tell you today," I say. "That's why I came early. Promise."

"Ugh," Beatrix says. "You told the new girl and not me. I looked so ridiculous."

I wince. "Sorry."

"I thought you liked doing dance together," says Beatrix. "I help you out all the time, as much as I can."

"You do help," I say. "But I'm still not any good. It's just not my thing."

Beatrix shrugs. "Fine. Do what you want."

From her voice, I know it's not fine. It's the opposite of fine. Her tone is friendly on the surface, but the undercurrent is dangerous, electric.

"Okay," I say. I wish we could get past this, skip forward to the good part of hanging out. I want to fill our plates at the nacho bar and see who's already down in the basement playing Ping-Pong.

"That girl is awful. What a weirdo," she says. "I can't believe you brought her to my house."

I feel tired. If I could, I would choose to hibernate for the rest of middle school.

"She's not awful," I say. "She seems nice."

Beatrix's eyes narrow. "She's a mess. Her skin is disgusting. If my face looked like that, my mom would *die*."

That is over the line, even for Beatrix. I should say something. I open my mouth, but then I snap it shut.

It feels like a teeter-totter moment. I think back to

what Mom said at dinner the other night. *Not having a place to sit at lunch is the worst thing possible for a seventh-grade girl.* That could be me, if Beatrix freezes me out. I can't let that happen again.

But no. That's not right.

"She didn't do anything wrong," I say. "She can't help her skin."

"And now you're sticking up for her," Beatrix says. "That's just great. Maybe she'll be your new best friend."

I can hear the hurt wrapped up in her words.

"Come on," I say. "That's not going to happen. Not in a million years."

Beatrix looks at me, waiting. All I want is for things between us to be easy again.

"Okay," I finally admit. "When I met her, she was wearing a hat that looks like a pumpkin. A *lumpy* pumpkin."

As soon as the words are out, I want to erase them. There's a hard feeling in my chest. I feel small and mean. And weak.

Beatrix screeches in delight. "A lumpy pumpkin? I don't believe it."

She is loud. I hope Hazel is no longer in the kitchen. I don't want her to hear us. My stomach smashes itself into a lump.

Happy again, Beatrix pulls on my sleeve. I still have a place to sit at lunch tomorrow. I still have a best friend.

A wave of relief bubbles up around the twist of guilt I feel about Hazel.

We head downstairs to the party.

I bite the skin on my thumb and tell myself it's worth it.

CHAPTER

7

Downstairs, I don't see Hazel anywhere. Maybe she left with her mom. Probably for the best. The image of Hazel smiling in her lumpy pumpkin hat floats in my mind. I hate what I said about Hazel's hat. I wish I hadn't said it. If I could, I'd launch my words past the Milky Way.

In the time we were upstairs, people had arrived. Voices and laughter swirl together, blending with the jazz coming from the three musicians playing in the living room. Bunches of peonies are arranged everywhere—Mrs. Bailey's favorite flower, always in single-color arrangements, which she says are more tasteful. In winter, she has to have them delivered from faraway places, but she says it's worth it.

Caterers with bow ties travel around the room, hoisting sparkling silver trays with small bites of food stacked on top. I've tried all kinds of foods at the Baileys', including lamb salad, scallop sashimi, and once even escargot, which means snail. It was the biggest mistake of my life.

Whenever Mrs. Bailey hosts a party, she devotes an entire notebook to it. She plans the menu, the decorations, the music. She even creates a lighting scheme. I've seen her snap when a chandelier is not dimmed properly. Beatrix told me that her mom thinks of a keyword and centers the entire party around it. But in my opinion, the keyword is always the same: "fancy."

Without being obvious, I scan the room for my parents. Mom holds Elsie on her hip. Elsie is tired, rubbing her eyes—but she manages to keep a good grip on her tiger purse.

Mom talks to a few people from her book club. Dad balances several appetizers on his plate and talks to Mr. Briggs, the retired railroad engineer. I don't see Conrad, but he's probably in the Bailey basement, watching the Ping-Pong battle take place.

Beatrix and I take the appetizers we are offered. My favorite is a teeny tiny chicken potpie that I eat in one bite. Everything is perfect and cute.

"Come on," says Beatrix. "Let's go downstairs."

When she opens the door, a burst of cheering comes from the basement. It sounds like the Ping-Pong tournament is in full swing. It's hard to see because so many people are clustered around the table. I wonder who is playing—probably Dexter and one of the other boys. At the beginning of the school year, Beatrix started acting like it was weird if girls wanted to play, especially if they were competitive over it. It didn't take long for all the girls to stop playing. Now we watch the boys. At the Christmas party, the whole night was spent whispering about which one of the high school boys was the best-looking. It's boring and not as fun as it was when we all played together.

I nod and say hi to a few girls from our grade. Beatrix and I squeeze in next to Zoe and Arshi, who lean against the wall.

Conrad is at one end of the table, swinging his paddle. The crowd blocks his opponent, but when I shift I see a flash of orange. It's Hazel in her pumpkin hat. And she's playing against my brother.

Beatrix has spotted her, too. She tilts her head sideways. "I thought that girl went home already."

Arshi pulls her eyes away from the table to glance at Beatrix. "Who is she?"

"She's actually fantastic," Zoe says, tossing her straight brown hair. "She's *serious*."

Beatrix pretends she doesn't hear.

"That's Hazel," I say. "She's new."

"She wasn't invited," Beatrix says.

Part of me wants to point out that technically she *was* invited, both because she is part of the neighborhood and

44

because Mrs. Bailey said so. Except that would make Beatrix madder. Besides, at this moment, what I want most is to watch Hazel play. Zoe is right: Hazel is good.

The boys pretend that the Ping-Pong table is a goof, but they all seem to keep careful track of the points that add up on the board. No one is supposed to be obvious about caring, but everyone pays attention to who is a winner and who is a loser.

Hazel is strong, but smart. Her game is quick and ruthless. Each flick of her wrist sends the ball in its intended direction. Conrad's skinny arms sprawl as he tries to keep up. He spends so much time working to receive Hazel's shots, he doesn't have a chance to be thoughtful about his responses. But Hazel is cool, unflappable. When she wins, the whole room breaks out in cheers. Except Beatrix, of course.

Conrad is smiling and shaking his head. He says something to Hazel that looks like *nice job*. I feel a little burst of pride for my brother. He may not be a good player, but he is a good sport.

He sees me and walks in our direction.

"Hey," he says.

Up close, I can see his hair is wet and his shirt sticks to him.

"Ugh, you're all sweaty," I say.

He acts like he's going to wipe his gross sweat on us, and we squeal and duck backward.

But Beatrix steps forward again. Giggling, she gives him a play shove. We used to always ignore Conrad when he was around, but at some point this year, she's started joking with him like this. I don't really like it.

She tosses her hair. "I can't believe you let her beat you, Conrad." Maybe I'm imagining it, but I think there's a slight emphasis on *her*. Hazel.

Conrad chuckles. "I didn't *let* her do anything. She's crushed a bunch of us. Her old school had an actual team for table tennis."

Beatrix twitches just slightly. Probably, someone who didn't know Beatrix well wouldn't see it—but I do. It reminds me of a pot on a stove, when the surface seems to flutter a second before it boils. She opens her mouth, like she's about to say something.

My thoughts whirl. I don't want to see Beatrix boil over. Especially about Hazel, who wouldn't even be at this party if it weren't for me and those meatballs.

"This is boring," I say. "Let's go back upstairs."

"Do what you want," Beatrix says coolly. "But I'm staying."

I lean against the wall next to her. I talk to Arshi about the basketball game she played yesterday. I talk to Zoe about her entry for the upcoming art show. I even try to get Beatrix interested in talking about some of the boys, but she doesn't want to. Her eyes stay on Hazel the whole time.

As we watch, I see some boys overdo it, smashing the ball across the table. They can't recover if there's a quick return. Other boys are more watchful, but maybe too cautious. But from what I can see, none of them is even close to being as good as Hazel. She's in her own league.

Time passes, and the caterers set up a dessert buffet on the table near the back wall of the basement. The Ping-Pong tournament pauses, and kids load up on cupcakes and brownie bites. Hazel makes a plate and comes over to us.

"Hi," she says. She turns to Arshi and Zoe, smiling. "I'm Hazel."

"You're so good at Ping-Pong," Arshi says sweetly.

"*So* good," Beatrix echoes, but her voice is sharp.

Hazel doesn't seem to notice. "Thanks," she says.

Zoe and Arshi introduce themselves, saying their whole names even though they are the only Zoe and Arshi in our whole town.

Beatrix looks at Hazel's plate. "*Wow.* You must really like dessert."

Hazel pauses, glancing at me like I can help. "Well, yeah," she says, like it's a trick question. "Doesn't everyone?"

Beatrix doesn't say anything. Zoe rattles the ice in her cup.

We're all silent until it feels too awkward and I have to say something.

"Hazel and her mom moved into Mrs. Johnston's house," I say.

Beatrix finally looks interested. "What about your dad?"

Hazel shrugs. "They split up a long time ago."

Beatrix's eyes narrow. "But does he live in Newford? Isn't that kind of far away?"

I'm not sure why Beatrix cares so much about Hazel's dad. We know plenty of kids in Willow Pond with divorced parents.

Hazel tugs at her earlobe. I feel a flash of anger at Beatrix. Obviously she doesn't like Hazel, which is fine. But there's no reason to make Hazel feel weird or uncomfortable.

Hazel takes a deep breath. "My dad's a scientist. He does important fieldwork and can be gone for months at a time. He goes to remote places where he can't leave or even call. So it doesn't matter where we live. He comes to see me whenever he can."

"What kind of science does he do?" I ask.

"All kinds," Hazel says firmly. "Right now he's assisting on a deep-sea dive where they are searching for the seven-armed octopus. Have you heard of it? It's very rare."

Beatrix glances at me, like I act as her personal science expert and can confirm whether it's true.

"I haven't heard of it," I say. "But the ocean is a big place."

"Hazel, come on!" Beatrix's brother Dexter calls.

Hazel shoves a tartlet in her mouth and heads back to the Ping-Pong table.

Beatrix watches her go. Her eyebrows pull together. "Did you believe her?"

"About the octopus?"

"About *everything*," she says. "I don't trust her one bit."

I frown. "Why would she lie?"

Beatrix shakes her head slowly. "I don't know. But I'm going to find out."

CHAPTER

8

Beatrix gets tired of hate-watching Ping-Pong, so we head upstairs. When we get there, Elsie spots us. She comes at us in her little stomping run, her arms outstretched. I think she is reaching for me, but at the last minute she swerves toward Beatrix, who scoops her up in a hug.

"Where were you, Bee-twix?" she asks, bottom lip poking out. "I was missing you."

Cheesecake streaks Elsie's face. I find a napkin and try to wipe her cheek, but she squirms.

"No, no," she says. "Eat brownies instead."

Beatrix grins. She adores my sister. When Elsie was born, Beatrix and I treated her like our doll. We changed her outfits and combed her hair until it shone. Elsie won't sit still for that anymore, but Beatrix thinks she's even more fun now.

"Let's find you some brownies," Beatrix agrees. Instead of walking, she bunny-hops to the dessert table, which makes Elsie giggle. When they get there, they stack brownies, tartlets, and cheesecake bites on a small plate.

We find a cozy corner to sit in. The party is coming to an end. Arshi's ajji, wearing blue jeans, a crisp sweater, and a bindi, comes over to say hi. Mr. Ramirez, Zoe's dad, is telling my dad a funny story. I can hear them laughing from across the room. One by one, parents call down the basement stairs to tell their kids it's time to go. Elsie munches another brownie.

"Do you want to try something different?" I ask. I hold up a tiny key lime tartlet.

Elsie shakes her head so hard, her curls bounce.

"They're so good, Elsie," says Beatrix, taking one from the plate. But when she bites it, half the filling slides off and lands on her sweater.

Elsie points at the mess. "Oops, Bee-twix!"

Mrs. Bailey happens to be walking by. When she sees us, her forehead creases in a frown. "Get some cold water on that right now, before the stain sets," she says to Beatrix.

Beatrix ignores her, bouncing Elsie in her arms.

Mrs. Bailey's smile pinches at the edges. "You're a mess," she says. "A hot mess."

She says it like she's joking, but I hear that electric current underneath—same as the one I heard earlier from Beatrix.

Mrs. Bailey sighs. She goes to say goodbye to Zoe's parents. Beatrix rolls her eyes and pops a mini cheesecake into her mouth.

"I get down now," says Elsie. When Beatrix sets her down, she runs straight to Dad, who is holding up her little red coat.

Beatrix rubs at the spot on her sweater. "I wish you could stay over tonight."

"Me too," I answer automatically, even though I'm already looking forward to my own bed.

Dad walks over, holding Elsie's hand. Conrad follows a step behind.

"Ooh," Dad says, snatching a tartlet from our plate. He chomps it, making *mmm* noises the whole time.

"Okay," he says. "I've got three kids rounded up. All we need now is Mom."

"She's over there," I say. Mom is deep in conversation with a woman with long, gray-streaked hair. Mrs. Bailey is talking with them, too. They're having one of those mom talks where everyone is supposedly saying goodbye, but it stretches out endlessly.

Dad attempts to put on Elsie's coat, but she is doing that trick where she goes limp. He looks up at me. "Can you go get Mom? Elsie's almost out of steam, and I think we need to head home."

Beatrix and I go over to the moms. When we get close, Mom glances up.

"Hey, girls," she says. "Did you meet our new neighbor— Sorry. I know you said your name is Astrid, but what should the kids call you?"

The woman's friendly smile seems familiar. I realize she must be Hazel's mom, except she looks a lot older than the moms in Willow Pond. She has long, curly gray hair. She's solid in a way that reminds me of a tree. Her necklace has a big purple stone in the middle, and she wears long turquoise earrings. Her style stands out, like Hazel's.

"Call me Astrid," she says.

Mom and Mrs. Bailey exchange a look. Mrs. Bailey tucks a piece of hair behind her ear.

"Let me explain," says Mrs. Bailey. "A few years back, we all agreed to always go by Mr. whoever or Mrs. whoever," she explained. "Kind of like not letting the kids have cell phones before high school or serving only organic milk. It just makes things easier to have everyone on the same page, parenting-wise."

Astrid's eyes widen a bit. She nods politely. "That does seem like it would make things . . . easier."

Mrs. Bailey beams. "Wonderful. Then it's settled."

"The thing is," Astrid continues, "I'm not a Mrs. Not now, not ever. And even if I were, I'd still want everyone to call me Astrid. That's my name."

Mrs. Bailey's smile clenches. Before she can say anything, a wave of noise interrupts. The last few kids have clomped up the basement stairs, and Hazel is at the center. Apparently, the Ping-Pong tournament is over. By the way she's grinning, I don't have to ask who won. Hazel sees us and heads our way.

"Hey, Astrid," she says. "I'm ready to go."

I can feel my eyes widen. When she said *everyone* called her Astrid, she meant everyone. Her own kid, too. I have never in my entire life known someone who called their mom by her first name. Mrs. Bailey's mouth is rounded in an O. Beatrix looks at me with her eyebrows raised high.

But Astrid doesn't seem to notice the reactions surrounding her.

"Thanks so much for letting us crash the party," Astrid says warmly. "Your home is lovely, and you were so gracious to allow us to wander in."

Mrs. Bailey's smile is frosty. "Of course. The whole neighborhood is always welcome."

"Roar!" shouts Elsie as she gallops through the kitchen, Dad chasing after. "Roar!"

"'Bye," Hazel says. "Guess I'll see you tomorrow."

Beatrix snaps her fingers like she just remembered something. "Wait a second! I have something for you! Stay here!" She races up the stairs.

Astrid beams at Hazel. "Glad you're already making friends. I'll wait outside as you say your goodbyes." She opens the door, and the winter air swirls in.

Beatrix comes down the steps, holding a small tube the color of an apricot. I know what it is—acne cream. A fancy one from France. At a sleepover last month, Beatrix and I tested it on our noses, even though neither of us had any zits. It smells heavenly.

I frown. Beatrix doesn't seem to like Hazel, so giving her a gift is weird. But then I realize what's happening. Pointing out Hazel's skin isn't a nice thing to do, especially not in front of everyone like this. It's a sneaky kind of mean . . . the kind of thing Beatrix does only when she thinks the adults won't notice. I've been best friends with Beatrix so long that she usually can't surprise me. But I'm not just surprised—I'm *shocked*.

Beatrix presses the tube into Hazel's hand. "This is what my mom got me for pimples, but I haven't had any yet. It's supposed to work magic on terrible skin. Why don't you take it?"

Hazel studies the tube. Her smile turns to confusion; then I think I see a spark of anger.

I hold my breath. Hazel's future at Willow Pond Middle School will be determined right here. I try to send her a brain wave. *Take the tube, don't say anything, don't react at all. The safest thing is to fly under Beatrix's radar. Don't make things hard on yourself.*

"Thanks," Hazel says finally. Politely.

"Anytime," says Beatrix in a twinkly voice that is secretly full of sharp, pointy edges.

Hazel's hand touches the doorknob, and I feel my breath loosen, my shoulders relax. She understands somehow that it's safer not to fight Beatrix.

But Hazel pauses, then turns around. This time she looks right at Mrs. Bailey.

"Thanks again for letting us come to your party," she says. "The food was delicious, and your home is really nice."

Mrs. Bailey smiles. It's a real smile this time, because Hazel is being polite, and Mrs. Bailey loves manners.

"That's very sweet of you, Hazel."

Hazel isn't finished. "I was so sorry I didn't see those grape jelly meatballs out with the rest of the food. They sure smelled good. I think maybe someone forgot to set them out."

My head snaps to the counter where the food is set out, buffet-style. I don't see Mom's meatballs. I frown, double-checking. They aren't there.

Mrs. Bailey's smile tightens. "We don't always have room to put out everything. You understand how it is."

"Oh yes," Hazel says, smiling widely. "I understand." She glances at me, as if checking to see if I heard. Then she turns and goes outside. The door clicks shut behind her.

ANIMAL FIELDWORK PROJECT

MS. DUPART

EXPLORATORY SCIENCE

SECOND SEMESTER

SIXTH PERIOD

PART

2

For social animals, give an example of how the group structure is enforced.

25 points

Queen bees do more than lay eggs. They also send out pheromones, chemical messages that the bees use to communicate certain messages such as "Danger!" or "Everything is okay!"

One interesting pheromone is queen mandibular pheromone. It says: "You are a bee that belongs to this hive."

If a bee does not smell right, the other bees think there is a threat. They will harm a bee that doesn't belong.

CHAPTER
9

Dad stands at the kitchen counter, piling a plate with his famous lemon waffles. He's whistling happily. I scowl. Dad is a morning person. I am not.

He hands me my plate, and I pull up a chair next to Conrad. Elsie gnaws on a sausage link. Her cheeks are sticky, and there are droplets of maple syrup in her curls. Two-year-olds have a way of throwing themselves into their food. I scoot my chair so I'm out of her reach.

Normally, lemon waffles are my favorite, but today I barely taste them. I keep replaying last night in my thoughts. I want to find the moment where it all went wrong, but there isn't one. Beatrix disliked Hazel immediately, and then things just got worse.

Mom comes into the kitchen, dressed for work. She rarely eats in the morning, and she never sits down. Instead, she drinks her coffee, unloads the dishwasher, checks messages on her phone. She's not a morning person, either.

"More sausage?" Dad says to us kids. "Orange juice? Or I could scramble an egg real fast."

Dad likes to make big breakfasts. Mom says it's because he works from home and doesn't have to rush out the door. I think it's because he likes to have us all together before the day begins.

"I'm okay," I say.

He looks at the three of us and decides Elsie is in need of the most help. He leans down for her. "Let's wash your face."

"No!" Elsie howls. "Tigers no wash faces!"

"Of course they do," Dad says reasonably. "They wash their faces in the river. But your river comes from our faucet."

Elsie looks suspicious, but she gives in. A few minutes later, I can hear them in the downstairs bathroom, splashing.

Mom catches my eye and smiles. "Ready for the new semester?"

I shrug. "Most of my classes are staying the same. Except science elective."

Mom grins. "Can't wait to hear about it."

Through the window, I see Mrs. Bailey's sleek black

SUV turn in to our driveway. I check the clock. They're five minutes early.

I push my plate aside. "Gotta go."

"Come here," says Mom. I walk over, and she wraps me in a hug.

Then she speaks quietly in my ear. "Keep an eye out for that new girl, Hazel. Remember that you're lucky to have been together with the same kids your whole life. Being new can be hard."

When I pull back, Mom's eyes are shiny. I know why she's emotional—she's thinking about how her family moved a lot when she was a kid. I can't imagine going to eight schools between kindergarten and the end of high school.

But at the same time, *Mom* can't imagine that being with the same kids since kindergarten has its own problems. Everyone knows me as one half of Beatrix-and-Meg. Sometimes if people see me by myself, they ask me immediately where Beatrix is, like we're a matched pair who always go together.

I step backward. "'Bye, everyone!"

From down the hall, Dad and Elsie yell "'bye." Conrad glances up from his cereal and barely has the energy to nod. I get it. He's not a morning person, either. I shrug on my fleece and head outside.

The morning is chilly, but Mrs. Bailey's SUV is a fully contained bubble of warmth, including the seats. Plus, her car is always spotless and smells like tangerines. It's nothing like my family's van, which is old and has stained seats, a lingering smell of milk, and Goldfish crackers crammed in unusual places. Dad always jokes that if we were somehow stranded in our van, we would have enough food to last a week.

After I fasten my seat belt, Beatrix hands me a purple cup. "We got your favorite."

Mrs. Bailey smiles. "It's cold, so we decided an Uncle Bean's run was necessary."

I sip my Vanilla Bean Scream, which is sweet and not too hot. I love having Uncle Bean's on school mornings. As much as I love my hot, sweet drink, there's something extra special about having it with Beatrix in homeroom. Matching Uncle Bean's cups is one of those special best-friends things that everyone can see.

Beatrix grins. Her cheeks are flushed, but I don't know if it's from the cold or from excitement.

"So," she says. "Remember that weird girl from yesterday?"

I lower my cup. She must be talking about Hazel. I hope we won't be calling her *weird girl*.

"What about her?"

"Apparently, her mom told Ryan's mom, who told Zoe's mom, who told *my* mom that in Newford, they had bees!" Beatrix's eyes are wide with the horror of it. "Is that not the grossest thing you've ever heard?"

I don't think it's gross. More like terrifying. I hate most

flying insects, especially ones that sting, and extra especially *bees*. Just thinking about bees makes me feel that outer-space, prickly feeling in my brain. I tell myself it is okay. There are no bees in the car. The bees are far away, in Newford.

"Their house had bees in it?" I ask.

Beatrix shakes her head. "Not random bees. They were in beehives, on the roof of their apartment building. That girl and her mom are beekeepers."

My heart beats fast. I've been stung only once, when I stepped on a bee at the pool. But still, I remember how it burned. I panicked, like I was crying without the sound coming out. Then I fainted. The idea of someone keeping bees around on purpose sounds ridiculous. *Dangerous.*

"And," Beatrix adds dramatically, "they're planning to move them here to Willow Pond."

"What?" I manage to squeak. "They can't do that. Can they?"

We're at a stoplight, and Mrs. Bailey glances over her shoulder. "Now, girls. Don't worry yourselves about it. Our town has laws and ordinances for this kind of thing. A neighborhood is no place for beehives. Think of all the children who live in our area!"

"I don't get it," Beatrix says. "Why would anyone want bees around?"

Mrs. Bailey shrugs her narrow shoulders. "For honey, I guess? Seems like it's easier to buy it at the store, like the rest of us."

"Remember when I got stung at the beach last summer?" Beatrix says to her mom. "You had to scrape the stinger out of me, which was so disgusting. I had to put ice on it for a whole hour."

I wiggle the toes on my right foot, remembering the way my sting had burned. My stomach decides to clench itself even more than it was already.

"Do you really think they'll bring them here?" I ask.

Beatrix smiles smugly. "Mom is going to take care of it. Right, Mom?"

Mrs. Bailey makes a clicking sound with her tongue. "Just imagine what it would do to property values."

She doesn't say any more, but I know what she means. Mrs. Bailey knows every person in our town. Once she calls them all, the chance of Hazel bringing bees to Willow Pond will be zero percent.

CHAPTER
10

Willow Pond Middle has block classes, which means that instead of having separate literature and social studies classes, they are combined into one. It's called literacy block. My other core class is math/science block. My first class of the day is literacy block with Mr. Thornton. Beatrix is in there, too.

Mr. Thornton goes through all the expectations for behavior, assignments, and tests—even though everything has stayed exactly the same. He says the class can think of it as a good opportunity to regroup. More like a good opportunity to be bored.

But I try to forgive Mr. Thornton, because he is a nice

teacher. He has curly brown hair, brown skin, and tons of freckles. He always wears plaid shirts. An interesting fact about Mr. Thornton is that he doesn't have a right arm. It stops right at his elbow. He says he doesn't miss it at all because that's how he was born. It's the kind of thing I thought would be a big deal because I might keep noticing it, but it turned out to be something I forget about most of the time.

There are only seven minutes left in the period when the classroom door opens. Mr. Nilsen, the seventh-grade counselor, is standing there, and Hazel is right behind him.

"I've got a new one for you," Mr. Nilsen says. "Meet Hazel."

"Welcome!" Mr. Thornton's voice makes it sound like a new student is the best, luckiest thing that could have happened at that moment. "Find a seat. And don't worry—I won't make you introduce yourself to the class. That only happens in movies and books anyway!"

A few kids laugh at that, and I smile a little, too. But Hazel keeps standing at the front of the class. Maybe she doesn't know where to sit. But it gives everyone the opportunity to look at her—and her outfit. A couple of kids snicker and shift in their seats.

Hazel wears yellow from head to toe: a yellow raincoat over a yellow sweater with black dots, blue leggings with yellow lightning bolts, and pulled up over the leggings are socks with fat yellow bees. Tiny yellow pom-poms dangle from her ears, and she is wearing yellow sneakers. Looking at her feels like standing on the surface of the sun.

"I don't mind introducing myself," she says. "My name is Hazel James, and I moved here from Newford. At my old school, I started lots of clubs. Stargazing, ultimate chess, geology explorers, culinary adventurers. I don't know if you guys have clubs here, but I'm hoping to start some."

Everyone in the class stares at her.

Beatrix mutters, "That's . . . *amazing.*" She says it in the way where she means the opposite.

"Does she think that's going to impress us?" whispers Zoe.

The back of my neck gets hot. I hope Hazel will sit down now, but she keeps talking. It's like she doesn't notice how quiet everyone is.

"I also love table tennis and beekeeping," Hazel says. She takes a deep breath, but before she can continue, Mr. Thornton interrupts her.

"Great, Hazel, thanks for that," Mr. Thornton says. "Go ahead and find a seat."

But Beatrix is raising her hand. "I have a question for Hazel, Mr. Thornton."

My stomach squeezes. I hope Beatrix won't ask about the bees. I feel jittery, on edge.

Mr. Thornton glances at the clock. "Okay. Quickly. If that's okay with you, Hazel."

Beatrix flicks her eyes at me, then smiles at Hazel.

"Can you tell us more about that octopus your dad is looking for? It sounds . . . *fascinating*."

Zoe giggles, and a few others do, too.

There's a way to be mean to someone right under a teacher's nose, and unfortunately Beatrix is a master of it. Everyone in the class can tell what's happening except Mr. Thornton and, maybe, Hazel.

Hazel smooths her hair. "The *Haliphron atlanticus* is a seven-armed octopus that is eleven feet long. My dad is on a submarine expedition, searching for it."

Beatrix raises her hand. "Have they found it yet?"

Hazel's expression tightens. "He's on a submarine. No calls or emails in or out for months."

Ryan Hong frowns, pushing his hands through his black, spiky hair. "I have a question. If it has seven arms, is it actually an *oct*opus? Wouldn't that be a *sept*opus?"

Everyone laughs, but Hazel's face is serious.

"Well, technically, it has an eighth arm. That arm is kept curled up in a special sac under its eye." Hazel shifts, looking uncomfortable for the first time. "The eighth arm is used for, um, fertilization?"

Ryan scrunches up his face. "Whoa! It uses its arm to fertilize things?"

The class explodes in laughter. Hazel's face reddens.

Mr. Thornton sighs. "All righty, I think that's just about enough. Go ahead, Hazel, you can grab a seat anywhere."

Hazel hesitates before taking an empty seat in the first row. I know it isn't nice, but I'm relieved that all the seats by me are taken. Beatrix smirks at Zoe, and I look down at my Uncle Bean's cup. Mr. Thornton walks from row to row, passing out homework.

"First bees and now octopuses. That girl is a walking zoo." Beatrix's voice is that perfect volume—too quiet for Mr. Thornton to hear but loud enough for the kids at the surrounding desks.

I feel everyone swivel to stare at Hazel, but I don't. Instead, I look down at my desk. My hands are in my lap, and I'm squeezing my thumbs hard so I don't start biting them.

This is all my fault. Beatrix hates Hazel because of me.

If I could, I'd go back in time and wouldn't bump into Hazel in the first place. Or if I couldn't erase that, at least I would be sure not to mention science elective. Because I think that's what upset Beatrix. If I hadn't spilled the beans to Hazel, Beatrix probably wouldn't have made a big deal about the new girl, even if she did seem a little weird. She would be regular-Beatrix, the one who loans people pencils and says, "You can keep it." The Beatrix who writes nice notes when a friend is feeling sad.

I want to tell her to stop acting this way, to just be normal. But I don't know how. My thumb finds its way to my mouth and I chew the skin there for the rest of class.

When the bell rings, I take my time putting away my pencil. I don't stand up until Hazel has a chance to leave class and melt into the crowded hallway.

"Come on," says Beatrix, and I hoist my backpack onto

my shoulder and follow her to the math/science hall. We always walk together.

We don't see Hazel in the hall, and I'm relieved. Beatrix goes to her class and I go to mine, which is my favorite class of the day. I smile for what feels like the first time since I got in the Baileys' car.

Getting Ms. Dupart for math/science block is one of the luckiest things that ever happened to me. She explains complicated things perfectly. She can also be dramatic, in a playful way, and she does things that make us laugh, even when we're learning a lot. Her classroom is full of interesting things in jars. She has models of every organ in the human body and even has a life-size skeleton Conrad told me is actually from a real dead body. I don't know if that's true. But I do know that Ms. Dupart says that all good scientists must have inquisitive minds and question everything.

The classroom is full of small two-person tables arranged roughly in rows. We sit with our lab partners, which means I am with Cora Wu, who wears purple glitter eyeglasses and has a sharp, angular haircut. Beatrix says Cora thinks she's better than everyone, but I think she's just a little shy.

As the bell rings, Ms. Dupart sweeps into the room. As always, her hair is in perfectly styled locs and she is wearing very high-heeled shoes. Today they are the exact color of ripe plums.

"Good morning, class. Today we'll be looking at the

syllabus and reviewing procedures and expectations. It's boring to me, it's boring to you, but it's school policy, so we will follow it."

I take in a deep breath and blow it out slowly. Somehow, I forgot that the first day of a new semester is always like this. Ms. Dupart goes through her slides one by one, explaining about lab notebooks, experiments, and expectations. Even Ms. Dupart can't make classroom rules interesting, especially when everyone knows them already. Classroom rules are easy.

The real rules of middle school are harder to learn— rules about where to sit, who to be friends with. How to act and what to wear. I don't have to make some of the decisions that other people do. Beatrix makes most of the rules about who sits at our table and who we hang out with. I've always been okay with that. Being best friends with Beatrix is like having a bubble around me that keeps me safe.

Of course, Beatrix comes with her own set of rules. I know most of them by heart. But switching to science elective meant breaking one. That's why I feel afraid. I never minded following Beatrix's rules before. But this year I feel out of balance with her, like she takes up more space in a room than I do.

"That's enough for the rules, I think," Ms. Dupart says. "Now I'm going to tell you a bit about the solar system, which is our next unit. When we wrap up our study, we will do a group project called Pageant of the Planets. Each group will present a different celestial body to the class. Music and dancing are optional but encouraged."

Cora catches my eye and grins. Ms. Dupart's class is so special. The other seventh-grade science classes are probably writing boring reports.

When the bell rings, I meet Beatrix in the hall, and we head for the lunchroom. Beatrix and I always bring our lunches. My working theory is that the cafeteria is the only place where people are willing to wait in a long line for terrible food.

Zoe and Arshi are already at our table. Beatrix flops on the seat dramatically. "That Ping-Pong girl is so, so weird," she says.

"Definitely," Zoe says, straightening her ponytail.

"What happened?" Arshi asks.

"She gave this weird speech about octopuses. She used the word 'fertilization.' So gross," Beatrix says. "And she loves bugs, too. Even grosser."

Arshi twists her gold necklace. "I heard about the bees, but I didn't know about the bugs."

Beatrix frowns. "Bees *are* bugs, Arshi. That's what I'm talking about."

I open my bag of chips and look around the lunchroom. Hazel is sitting with a group of girls who are all really quiet and good at school. Hazel isn't talking, though—she's reading a book. But at least she has someone to sit with.

When the bell rings, Beatrix, Arshi, Zoe, and I head to

the locker room. We have PE at the same time, but Beatrix and Zoe have Coach Alinaghi, who also teaches dance elective. She is the best PE teacher. Her class does yoga, kickball, and creative relays. Arshi and I are stuck with Coach Pruett. Our class does only two things: calisthenics and running. We never play games. At least I have Arshi as my partner.

School policy or not, Coach Pruett does not believe in using a whole class period to talk about expectations. He believes in sweat. Finally, after an hour of torture, we are excused. I hurry to the locker room.

Last semester, I never rushed, because dance elective is right next door to the gym. Besides, I was never in a big hurry to get there. But science elective is on the other side of the school. I spin my lock, messing up the combination a few times. As much as I'm looking forward to science elective, I also feel nervous. It's like I can still hear Beatrix's voice in my ear, her comment about me being best friends with Hazel.

Finally, my locker opens. I change quickly and sling my backpack over my shoulder. I tell myself I'm okay. Science elective is a big class, and my plan is to avoid Hazel, no matter what.

CHAPTER

11

I make it to the classroom before the bell, but Ms. Dupart isn't there yet. Some kids stand around chatting, and some are already in their seats. The chair that I sit in during math/science block already has a blond boy sitting in it, talking loudly about the video game he played last weekend. Logically, I know that seat doesn't belong to me, but it still feels strange to see someone else in it.

I spot an open seat next to an eighth-grade girl with dark-brown hair and lots of freckles. But when I get there, she puts her arm across it.

"This seat is saved," she informs me.

The room is filling fast, but I see a spot next to Ryan.

"Is someone sitting here already?" I ask.

Ryan blinks his long, straight eyelashes, looking apologetic. "Alfredo. He had to go back to literacy block to get his folder."

Great. Just great.

And then, in the back corner, I see an empty table with two open seats. I hurry over and put down my backpack before anyone else can claim it.

But then I realize something. Hazel isn't here yet. When she shows up, she'll take the last empty spot—the one next to me. In my other class with Ms. Dupart, my seatmate is my lab partner, too. I can't let that happen.

I glance around the room, but every seat is taken. I don't know what to do, but I have to find somewhere else to sit. There's no way I can be partners with Hazel. Beatrix would make such a big deal about it. That wouldn't be good. Not for me and definitely not for Hazel.

I pick up my chair and drag it over to a table with two girls, both eighth graders. One has curly brown hair and glasses; the other has short red hair that's even brighter than Elsie's.

"Can I sit with you?" I ask, thinking quickly. "There's—um—a draft over there."

The girls shrug and slide their chairs so I can squeeze in.

Ms. Dupart strides through the door and closes it firmly behind her. The room quiets immediately. She's one of those teachers who knows how to be in charge without saying a word.

"Good afternoon, class, and welcome to the second

semester of science elective. Many of you are continuing from first semester, when the class was restricted to eighth graders. But this year, for the first time, we have some select seventh-grade students joining us. Welcome. Don't worry—you'll catch up quickly." She glances at me and smiles.

"Now I know you've been reviewing rules and expectations all day," she says.

There's some nodding and light grumbling. The eighth grader next to me sighs. It's the last class of the day, and everyone is tired of hearing the rules. I feel my shoulders slump. I've been looking forward to this class for so long, and it's going to be boring.

Her eyes twinkle. "But we will not be doing that."

I sit up straight. I knew this class would be good.

"Instead of revisiting rules and expectations during class time, I will distribute a handout for you to study and memorize. Quiz tomorrow, and I expect one hundred percent from everyone."

I write a note in my planner: *Study.*

"As you know, this is a class where I expect more in general. We move at a rapid pace, and much of your work is self-directed. My expectation is that zero behavior problems will exist. Most of you were in this class first semester, except for our seventh graders—"

The classroom door opens. It's Hazel. Some of the eighth graders haven't seen her yet, and I can tell they are noticing her outfit. I feel bad for Hazel, but I'm also *mad* at her. Maybe that's unfair, but what was she thinking, wearing weird clothes on her first day of school?

"Sorry," Hazel says, face flushed. "I got lost—"

"You must be Hazel," Ms. Dupart says. "I like your earrings."

Hazel reaches up to her ears and feels the yellow pom-poms. "Thanks."

Ms. Dupart gestures to the empty table. "Find a seat anywhere."

Thankfully, Hazel does not introduce herself this time. She heads to the empty table and sits down. But Ms. Dupart frowns, like she's noticing that the other chair is missing. She scans the room until she sees me with the eighth graders.

"One of you needs to move to the other table," she says.

I look down at my planner again. I'm not sure what the probability works out to, but maybe there's some chance that one of the other girls will move to Hazel's table. Maybe one in a thousand. But when I lift my eyes and sneak a glance at them, they are both glaring at me.

"We're not moving," the girl closest to me whispers.

"I don't care who it is, but it needs to happen now," Ms. Dupart says. Her tone is calm but serious. "We don't have time for this."

It's a reminder about what she said before. Zero behavior problems. I stand and gather my things. Everyone is watching me. I can feel their eyes. I pull my chair with me, and it makes a scraping sound across the floor.

"Sorry," I mutter. I maneuver the chair until it's next to Hazel, and then I sit down.

"Hi," she whispers.

Ms. Dupart nods crisply. "I'm glad we're all set. Everyone: look next to you, because that is your partner for the entire semester. You will research together, analyze data, and form conclusions. All great achievements in science have resulted from collaborations. Treat your partner wisely."

I look at Hazel, and she's smiling at me—that same friendly smile from yesterday, which only makes me feel worse. Hazel seems okay, maybe even better than okay. She likes science too, and in another dimension maybe we could be friends. But in this dimension, I'm best friends with Beatrix. When Beatrix makes up her mind, there's no way to change it. And Beatrix does not like Hazel one bit.

"Let's talk about our project for the semester." Ms. Dupart opens a slideshow and begins to click through. Normally I would be excited about this, but it feels like my thoughts are crowding in. I bite the skin by my thumb, trying to imagine a way to get out of being partners with Hazel.

Even though I'm distracted, it's impossible to ignore Ms. Dupart. She explains that our science elective is considered *exploratory*. We don't have to follow any set curriculum. This means that as a class, we get to decide what topics to cover.

Slides appear with photos of projects from previous years. One picture shows a line of rockets, ready to launch. Another shows two kids dressed up as an amoeba. I sigh. In all the pictures, kids are happy, which somehow makes me more miserable. This is supposed to be fun. Why did I have to get partnered with Hazel?

"Now, as you remember: last semester, our focus was lab work and we studied chemistry. This semester, our focus is fieldwork. This means you will collect data outside the classroom," says Ms. Dupart. She switches to a new slide with only two words.

GEOLOGY

BIOLOGY (ANIMALS)

"At the end of first semester, I polled the class for ideas on what we would study next. These are the two categories with the most votes," Ms. Dupart says. "Everyone tear off a half sheet of paper and write down your vote."

Hazel grins at me. "Definitely vote for biology," she whispers. "I have an awesome idea."

A jolt of anger runs through me. She's only known me since yesterday, and I don't even want her as a partner. Now she's pushing her idea on me. It's like I have a sign on my head saying Go Ahead, Push Me Around. Maybe I would let that kind of comment slide with Beatrix, but that's different. We've known each other since kindergarten. I've known Hazel less than twenty-four hours. She may be my partner, but she's not in charge of me.

"Don't tell me what to do," I say evenly. "I don't like being bossed around."

Hazel blinks fast and then looks down at her paper. Maybe that wasn't fair of me, but this class is supposed to be mine. The last thing I need is someone taking over. I look at the blank paper and try to decide. If Hazel hadn't said anything, I might have voted for biology. But now I scribble *geology* and pass my paper to the front.

As Ms. Dupart gets the ballots, she sorts them into two stacks. By the time she finishes, one pile is about six times larger than the other. *Geology. Please be geology.*

"It's decided," says Ms. Dupart. "In a landslide. We will be studying animals for our fieldwork semester. Welcome to Exploratory Biology."

The class rustles in excitement, but I sink in my chair. I hear Ryan say, "*Yes!*"

The final bell rings. School is over.

Hazel turns to me. "Sorry if I bossed you."

"It's fine," I say, jamming my planner and pencil case into my backpack.

"Do you want to hear my idea?" she asks.

Her face is hopeful and excited. I know I'm supposed to be nice to her, because being new is hard. But right now, I'm mad. I'm mad at her for telling me what to do. I'm also mad at myself for being the kind of person who can be bossed around.

"Not really," I say. Her mouth turns down. It's brief, but it's there.

"Oh," she says. "Okay."

"Sorry," I say. "I have to go." I head to the door and don't look back.

When I get outside, I automatically look for Mrs. Bailey's car, but then I remember it's Monday. Beatrix has dance right after school, so Dad usually picks me up. But instead of his van, Mom's Camry pulls into the parking lot.

I open the door and get in.

"My call got canceled, so I thought I'd come get you," she says. "How was your day?"

"Terrible," I answer. "Hazel is my partner for science elective."

"Terrible?" Mom asks. "She seemed so sweet yesterday, I wanted to give her a hug."

I shake my head. "No, Mom. She's just weird. You should have seen what she was wearing." An angry wave crashes over me. I don't know why Hazel had to wear that yellow outfit. It's like she wants people to pick on her.

Mom's mouth presses into a line. "Be nice, Meg. Maybe kids dress differently at her old school."

I don't say anything. Mom thinks being nice solves everything. But I'm tired of it. Beatrix tells me what to do.

Mom tells me what to do. And even weird Hazel tried to tell me what to do.

"The thing is, Meg, you don't understand how hard it is to move like she did, right in the middle of seventh grade," Mom says. "You are lucky because you know everyone in Willow Pond. And you have a best friend you've known forever."

I shrug, frustrated. I don't feel lucky at all.

"Maybe you and Beatrix can reach out to Hazel, show her around," Mom continues. "Try to see things from her point of view."

"Beatrix doesn't like her, either," I snap. "So don't think that we're all going to be best friends."

Mom gives me a look that means I should watch my tone.

"I would never want you to choose between friends," Mom continues. "I know how close you and Beatrix are."

Something about the way she says it makes me think she isn't finished.

"But?" I ask.

"But," she says gently, "it wouldn't kill you to be nice."

She pulls into our driveway and parks. Sighing deeply, she turns to me.

"When I started that new school, someone stole my backpack on the very first day," she says.

My eyebrows pop up. "They did?"

She nods. "I didn't want to report it, but someone turned it in. It had been in the boys' locker room."

"Ugh," I say. Mom always talks about how hard moving in middle school was, but this is the first time she's ever given me details.

Mom nods. "I had no idea where to sit at lunch, so I hid in the bathroom and ate my lunch there."

My mouth drops open. Mom, who is paranoid about germs, actually *ate food* while standing in a *public bathroom*. I check her face, but she's not joking.

"Mom," I say. "That's even grosser than the boys' locker room."

Mom gives me a sharp look. "What's *gross* is the way people can be so unkind to each other. You have no idea, Meg, because it's never happened to you."

Mom doesn't get mad often, but she's mad now. She gets out of the car and closes the door hard behind her. Not quite a slam but close. The conversation is over. I feel like I failed some sort of test.

For a minute, I sit by myself in the car. I feel bad for twelve-year-old Mom, who was lonely and scared in a new middle school. I don't want Hazel to feel that way. But at the same time, I don't want to do something that makes Beatrix *really* mad.

I'm stuck. And I have no idea how to fix it.

CHAPTER 12

Mom and I avoid each other the rest of the night. Dad's on a deadline, working upstairs in his office. Mom takes Conrad to music practice, puts Elsie to bed, and then goes to pick up Conrad. I'm not sure if she's mad or hurt. Maybe both. I'm confused. I don't like feeling far away from Mom, but sometimes I don't know how to talk to her.

The next morning, before she leaves for work, she catches me in a hug.

When she pulls back, she brushes a stray hair from my forehead. "Sorry about yesterday. I know you'll do the right thing."

She kisses my forehead, grabs her coffee, and rushes out the door. I watch her go. All I can think is that I don't know what the right thing is. If I did, then it would be easier.

I finish my cereal. Elsie is quietly dumping her bowl of applesauce onto her place mat, slowly spreading it with her fingers. Dad is pouring himself another cup of coffee, looking relaxed.

"Dad, remember? You're driving Beatrix and me this morning?"

He looks at me blankly. "But it's Tuesday."

"Because Mrs. Bailey has a morning meeting," I say to jog his memory.

"Oops," Dad says. There's an edge of panic to his voice. "Can you get Elsie in the car for me?"

I put my bowl in the sink. Elsie lets me wipe her hands, which is a miracle. I scoop her up, and we walk to the garage. But when I try to help her with her car-seat straps, she scowls.

"I do *myself*," she insists, pushing my hands away from hers. Her tiny fingers struggle to make the clip connect. It's adorable yet depressing to watch her work so hard at something that would take me about two seconds. Finally, she pushes the clip all the way in. She's so proud, her grin takes up her whole face.

"Good job," I say. The lower clips are a lot harder, and she lets me manage those.

When we get to Beatrix's house, she is waiting on the porch.

"Thanks for taking me today, Mr. Garrison," she says. "Hey, Meg. Hi, Elsie."

"Bee-twix!" Elsie shouts, holding out her hands in awe, like Beatrix is some sort of celebrity. On our turns to drive, we don't ever stop at Uncle Bean's, but at least we have Elsie.

Beatrix holds Elsie's hands and grins.

"They're sticky," I warn her.

"It's fine," she says. "How was science elective?"

I look at her carefully to see if there's mean hidden in her voice, but she seems to be asking in a normal way. I don't know how much to tell her, but if the last week has taught me anything, it's that hiding something from Beatrix is a bad idea. Dad, in the front seat, sips his coffee and listens to his favorite podcast.

"It seems okay, but I got Hazel for a partner," I say.

Beatrix makes a face. "Yuck."

"Yuck!" Elsie repeats. "Yuck, yuck, yucky."

Beatrix giggles. "Yucky Hazel."

The edge is in her voice again. I don't know why she has to make such a big deal about Hazel.

"Yucky Hazel," Elsie repeats.

"Don't say that," I tell her.

Beatrix leans toward Elsie. "Yucky science—right, Elsie?"

Elsie claps her hands. "Yucky science!"

Anger flares inside me. Elsie is *my* little sister. Beatrix shouldn't say that to her.

"Science isn't yucky," I tell Elsie. "Science is nice."

Beatrix shakes her head playfully, grinning at Elsie like it's a joke. "No way. We don't like science. Dance is nice. Dance is *fancy*."

"Tigers are fancy," Elsie says. "Tigers are nice. I like tigers!"

I'm burning inside, but I keep it to myself. Beatrix and I are quiet the rest of the ride. Dad drives through the drop-off loop, and Beatrix and I climb out of the car. I see Mrs. Bailey's SUV parked at the end of the drop-off loop. Technically, it isn't allowed, but Mrs. Bailey parks there all the time.

Beatrix sees me noticing.

"Another meeting for the big fundraiser," she says. "I think."

Mrs. Bailey is in charge of the parent-teacher organization. She's on every committee, but her specialty is fundraising. She says it's because she knows the whole town, but Beatrix says it's because no one can say no to Mrs. Bailey. That's probably what will happen with the bees, too, I realize. I shudder, but it's not from the cold.

"Let's go," says Beatrix. We walk inside the building.

I want to talk to Beatrix about what happened in the car. I hate that she brought Elsie into whatever is happening with Beatrix, Hazel, and me. I can tell Beatrix is angry, but it's buried deep inside. If we could talk about it, maybe it would be better. But I'm afraid of what she'll say—what she'll do. I don't say a thing, and neither does she.

But when we walk to class, it feels normal. Beatrix asks me a question about the homework, and it's like we can pretend this morning never happened. I see Hazel during literacy block, but she rushes out of the room as soon as the bell rings. She isn't in the lunchroom at all. An image flashes in my head of Mom as a kid, eating in the bathroom. I hope Hazel isn't hiding somewhere.

After I run the mile in PE, which I hate, I'm on my way to science elective again. I manage to get there early, and Hazel isn't at our table yet. When I open my planner, the first thing I see is the reminder to study. I completely forgot. My heart pounds. I pull out yesterday's handout and try to memorize as fast as I can.

The bell rings, but Ms. Dupart isn't there. Neither is Hazel.

I keep rereading the study sheet. I want to do well on today's quiz so Ms. Dupart feels like she made the right choice to let me take the class.

Finally, the sixth-grade counselor, Ms. Yates, shows up. She's holding a stack of papers.

"I'm covering for Ms. Dupart because she's in a meeting," she says. "But she told me to hand out these quizzes. Put your notebooks and papers away."

I take one last glance at the handout before shoving it into my backpack.

Everything is fresh in my brain, so the quiz isn't too bad. There's only one question I can't answer. I stare at my paper, willing the words to flow magically out of my pencil. Then the door opens, and Ms. Dupart comes back to class. Ms. Yates nods at her and leaves.

"Time's up," Ms. Dupart says. Her seafoam-green heels click as she walks around the room, collecting the papers. She tidies the pile with crisp, businesslike movements.

She leans against the desk. She's pretty old, I realize. Usually it doesn't seem that way, because her face is so lively. But now she seems all knotted up.

"I'm going to make an announcement, and I won't use class time to repeat it or elaborate further, so I need you to please pay attention."

Kids glance at one another. No one knows what's happening, but it seems serious.

Ms. Dupart takes in a deep breath. "Each one of you belongs here. Every single one. I have been at this school for thirty-seven years, and I have an outstanding track record. My reward for this is the ability to pick and choose the members of this class. If you have a seat here, you've earned it."

The door opens, and Hazel comes in. She walks quickly, not making eye contact with anyone. She slides into her seat next to me and stares straight ahead.

"All right," says Ms. Dupart. "That's all I have to say.

Take a few minutes to talk with your partners, as you will be picking the animal for your fieldwork study today."

Hazel looks down at her desk, eyes wide open, like she's trying not to cry.

I lean toward her. "Are you okay?"

She wipes her eyes before she looks at me. "Did your parents complain to the school about me being in this class?"

I'm shocked. "No! They wouldn't do that!"

She frowns. "Who else would it be? I don't know anyone else in here except Ryan, and we haven't exactly talked."

We both glance at Ryan, who is grinning, as usual, and leaning so far back in his seat that I'm surprised it hasn't tipped over. Hazel and I exchange a look. Ryan thought the seven-armed octopus was funny. He wouldn't complain about Hazel. But who would?

"What did they say at the meeting *exactly*?"

Hazel blew out a deep breath. "Someone said I'm new so I shouldn't be in this class—because I might not be academically qualified or something."

I can't believe it. "That's not okay."

Hazel manages a small smile. "Yeah. Ms. Dupart was so mad, I thought flames might shoot out of her ears. She's seen the research I do outside of school."

I'm impressed. I wish I were doing research outside of school, too. "You do research outside of school? Is it with your dad?"

"*No*," she says quickly. She rubs at her ear. "Not with him. On my own."

"Well, don't worry about it," I say. "She knows you're supposed to be here. And before you came back, she told everyone that we are all here for a reason. So don't be upset."

"All right," Ms. Dupart says. She has some of her twinkle back. "I need one member of each team to come to the front of the class."

Hazel glances at me. She wants to do it, I can tell.

"Go ahead," I say. It's the least I can do.

Ms. Dupart arranges Hazel and the other kids as they go up. Eventually, they're all standing in a row shoulder to shoulder, facing those of us left at the tables. Then Ms. Dupart uses blue painter's tape to stick index cards to the whiteboard behind the row of kids. The cards are labeled with words, but I can't read them from here.

Ryan is at the front of the class, too. He turns his head sideways in slow motion, trying to see the board without being obvious. Ms. Dupart notices, of course, and acts like she's smacking him on the shoulder with the roll of tape. He laughs.

"No peeking," she says, sounding half-amused, half-stern. "Stay facing your classmates."

After Ms. Dupart tapes all the cards, she stands in front of the class.

"Some of you may wonder what we are doing. We are not doing arts and crafts time, although Ms. Dupart loves herself some arts and crafts when it's time for weekend relaxation. But today is not about relaxation. Today is about science."

If every teacher in the world had a voice like Ms. Dupart, kids would learn a whole lot more. She has an intense way of speaking that makes me wonder what will happen next. It's a very good teacher trick.

"You will remember that the animal kingdom is sub-divided into phyla and then into classes. For our purposes today, we are concerned with these."

She finds a part of the board not covered with index cards and writes seven classes.

CLASSES*
1. MAMMALS
2. BIRDS
3. AMPHIBIANS
4. REPTILES
5. INSECTS
6. CRUSTACEANS
7. ARACHNIDS

*THIS IS NOT ALL OF THEM, BUT IT IS GOOD
ENOUGH FOR OUR PURPOSES TODAY.

When she's done making the list, she underlines it. "Now," she continues. "There are only two cards for each order. That means that two groups will study mammals, two will study arachnids, and so on. Within that order, you may choose a species to study. But there can be no duplicates. First come, first served."

Aniyah, one of the eighth-grade girls I tried to sit next to yesterday, raises her hand. "But what if more than two groups want to pick mammals?"

Ms. Dupart sighs, shaking her head. "There are two cards for mammals, which means two projects on mammals. I have learned that if I do not ensure a variety of projects, I will receive *fourteen* projects on mammals."

That's because mammals are the *cute* ones. Cute is good. I make eye contact with Hazel and nod, sending her a message: *pick mammals*. We could study squirrels, or rabbits, or the deer that live in the woods behind my house. Or even the raccoons that make Dad crazy when they steal from our garbage can. I mouth the words to her. *Pick mammals.*

Hazel grins and gives me a thumbs-up to say *message received*. I lean back in my chair.

"Now," Ms. Dupart continues. "I do not have anything against mammals, being one myself. But I find the idea of fourteen projects on mammals to be extremely—what is the word? *Boring.* The word is 'boring.'"

I'm hoping Hazel will be quick enough. If not, I guess birds would be okay.

Ms. Dupart holds up a small bell. "When I ring this

bell, the students at the front of the class may turn toward the whiteboard and select a card. Once a card is selected, it cannot be returned. First come, first served. No pushing, and watch the elbows."

She raises the bell in the air.

When it rings, fourteen kids rush the whiteboard. Hazel makes it there first. Arms fly and shoulders bump. Those of us in our seats laugh and clap. There is such a knot of people that I can see only the top of Hazel's blond head. Finally, she emerges from the scuffle, flushed and triumphant.

Beaming, she crosses to our table and holds out the card.

I smile back, reaching for it. But when I see, I frown. The card doesn't say mammals. It doesn't say birds.

Insects.

Our project is going to be about *insects*.

I look back at the board to see if there are any left, but they've all been claimed. And Ms. Dupart said no switching topics.

"I said to pick mammals!" I say.

Hazel's grin fades. "Oh. I didn't understand. I thought we could study my honey bees."

"*Bees?*" I ask. This is a nightmare. "But I'm afraid of bees. I'm terrified of them."

Hazel makes a *ffffft* sound. "There's nothing to be afraid of! Honey bee stings are rare. Besides, I have all the protective equipment we need. It's going to be absolutely perfect!"

She jumps up and goes to tell Ms. Dupart our topic. I don't have a chance to argue. Or a chance to suggest something else. I slump in my seat. Mom would say "Be nice," but I don't see how I can. Hazel said it would be absolutely perfect. But studying bees, with Hazel as a partner, is going to be perfectly awful.

CHAPTER
13

After school, Beatrix and I meet at our corner. The sky is bright blue and the sun is shining, with a hint of a breeze. It's definitely winter, but it's like I can feel spring peeking through. We pick up Bart and Lola, who are jumping with excitement. Then we make our familiar loop back to the middle school.

For the first time in two days, Beatrix is acting normal. She hasn't mentioned anything about science elective or Hazel. She hands me Lola's leash so she can show me what they're working on in dance class.

"That's so good," I say when she finishes. She's smiling her biggest smile—the one that makes her cheeks push up high. It's a different smile from the "pretty" one she does in photos. Seeing her this way reminds me of elementary school days, and I feel a rush of happiness for my friend. I'm glad she has something she loves so much.

Lola hunches, choosing this moment to do her business. I pull out a bag and pick it up. Beatrix doesn't stop pirouetting until I double-knot the bag. She takes Lola back, and we head over to the trash can before we turn toward home.

"So," Beatrix says casually. "Was anything different in science elective today?"

I wrinkle my head, thinking. "Not really different. We picked our research topics. I wanted mammals, but Hazel picked insects . . ."

When I see the surprise on her face, I stop.

"Hazel's in there?" she asks.

"Yeah," I say slowly. "You know she's in there." I don't get it. She made such a big deal about Hazel being my science buddy, and now she's acting surprised about Hazel and me being in class together.

"I mean—" Beatrix starts, then stops. "*Still?*"

"Why wouldn't she?" I ask. Then I understand. "Is that what your mom's meeting was about? Hazel being in science elective?"

Beatrix narrows her eyes at me. "The meeting wasn't specifically *about* that. It came up, because it's not exactly fair that someone who hasn't even been at our school gets to take an ultracompetitive elective. So Mrs. Jensen said she'd look into it."

The wind gusts, traveling through my jacket. The spring feeling from before is gone. It's like I can feel every frozen bone in my skeleton. Maybe I shouldn't be surprised that our principal listened to Beatrix's mom, but I am.

I pull my hood around my ears. "She may not have been at Willow Pond, but she's serious about science. She does actual research on her own, outside of school."

Beatrix waves her hand as if she can make it go away.

"Fine," she says. "It's not about Hazel anyway. It's about being fair. Because lots of kids want to take that elective but can't. She didn't even live here until a few days ago."

I don't know what to say. All I can think of is Hazel's face, trying not to cry.

"I shouldn't have told you," Beatrix says. "I might not even have remembered it right, about my mom bringing it up. Probably someone else said it first."

I wish I could believe her. I am furious with Mrs. Jensen for listening to Mrs. Bailey about Hazel. But I am also one-hundred-percent happy that Hazel has Ms. Dupart on her side.

"Anyway," Beatrix says. "How is it going? Did you say you picked your topic?"

"Sort of," I say. "Hazel actually was the one who picked."

Beatrix rolls her eyes. "Figures. Is it on the seven-armed octopus?"

"Worse. Bees." My insides twist when I think of it.

Beatrix gasps. "But you're super afraid of bees! You always have been."

I grimace. "I hate them. And the thought of them living in a hive, crawling all over one another . . . It gives me the creeps. Every time I think about it, I feel like I'm going to faint."

Beatrix's eyes widen. "That's not okay, Meg. You really could faint from it—you have before. It's not fair to make you do a school project on them."

"I don't know what to do," I say.

Beatrix taps a finger against her chin. "Hopefully, you won't have to do anything. I know my mom is trying to block them. If they aren't here, you won't be able to study them, right?"

I nod. Honestly, that would solve everything.

"But just in case, you should have another plan," she says. "Why don't you tell Ms. Dupart that you have a major fear of bees and need to switch to a different project? Maybe even say you're allergic. She doesn't have to know that you aren't. You still have a serious medical reason for not doing it."

"Maybe that would work," I say. "But Hazel would be sad."

Beatrix thinks for a second. "But if you do the bee

project, won't *you* feel sad? What if you faint again? You have to tell Ms. Dupart that you're *terrified* of bees. That's not anything against Hazel."

As I listen to Beatrix talk, I feel relieved. She's right. I shouldn't have to feel so scared about a school project. Maybe if Hazel wasn't so stubborn, she would have listened when I told her how I felt about the bees. It's not exactly fair that I didn't get to choose. And at this point, there's no way I could convince her to pick a different insect. She would never agree to that.

Maybe this is what's fair to Hazel and to me. I'll talk to Ms. Dupart tomorrow.

The next morning, Dad drives us through the drop-off line.

"Bye-bye!" Elsie shouts as we get out of the car.

"Good luck," Beatrix says. She knows what I'm going to do.

I walk to the math/science hall. When I get to Ms. Dupart's classroom, I hesitate. But she sees me standing there.

"Come on in," she says.

She's been writing notes on the board for her first-period class. Funky glasses are perched on her nose, and her high heels are flamingo pink.

It's warm in her classroom, and I start to feel sweaty. I take a deep breath.

"I'm sorry to bother you, but the thing is—I don't think I can be partners with Hazel." The words come out in a rush.

Ms. Dupart's eyebrows draw together, but she keeps writing on the board. "Good morning, Meg."

"Um," I say. "Good morning."

I wait to see if Ms. Dupart will say something else, but she doesn't.

"The thing is, Hazel really wants to do bees as her project, but I am terrified of them." My throat tightens at the thought of it.

"I see," says Ms. Dupart, not looking up. "Allergy?"

I pause for a moment, thinking of Beatrix's suggestion. But I can't lie to Ms. Dupart. Besides, what if she ever mentioned it to my parents? I'd be in so much trouble.

"I assume any allergies would be documented on your medical card," she says.

"Nothing like that," I say. "But I've been afraid of them since I was little."

Ms. Dupart lowers her glasses and looks at me. "I see."

We stand there for a minute, and I start to squirm.

"Meg," she says. "I recommended you for this class because you show great promise. You have a quick, investigative mind. I believe you may make a significant contribution to the field, if you choose to pursue science as a career."

My cheeks flush. I know Ms. Dupart likes me, or I wouldn't be in science elective. But those words are something else. I run them over in my mind. A significant contribution to the field? That feels important. Special.

"Now, if you don't want to work on bees, you can talk that over with Hazel," Ms. Dupart says. "But as a scientist, you should consider facing that fear. Study the bees not *in spite* of the fear but *because* of it."

I frown. "What do you mean?"

Ms. Dupart scrunches her forehead, like she's trying to find the best way to explain it. "Many people handle their fears by avoiding what scares them. But as a scientist, you have a responsibility to do the opposite. Get close to the thing that frightens you. Look it in the eye, ask the questions, find the answers. After a while, you may find your fear has been replaced by curiosity."

Another idea flashes in my head.

"But the thing is, I don't want to hold Hazel back. She knows so much about bees already," I say.

"Wonderful," Ms. Dupart says.

"But I don't know anything about them," I continue. "On purpose. Because I don't like them."

"Also wonderful," Ms. Dupart says. When she sees me looking confused, she smiles. "Hazel is going to come to this project with a set of preconceived ideas. That means that she already has some guesses about what she will see. She's already predicting what will happen."

I nod, glad Ms. Dupart understands what I'm saying. Hazel already knows so much about bees. I'll never catch up. Thoughts of what else I could study begin to cram my brain. Fireflies won't work in the winter. Maybe butterflies.

But Ms. Dupart interrupts my thoughts. "You have something else—something just as good. Maybe better," Ms. Dupart says. "You'll be able to observe with fresh eyes. It's a wonderful opportunity, Meg."

My hopes crash-land back to Earth.

Ms. Dupart pats my hand. "I'm so excited to see what the two of you come up with."

In other words, I'm stuck. I turn to go, but Ms. Dupart's voice stops me.

"Meg?"

I turn around. Maybe Ms. Dupart somehow changed her mind in the last five seconds. "Yes?"

Ms. Dupart looks thoughtful. "I hope you'll stick with the bees. And with Hazel. I have a feeling you have a lot you can learn from each other."

Disappointment curls in my stomach. I nod, then walk out the door. If I hurry, I can meet Beatrix before the bell rings.

CHAPTER
14

On Friday, when I walk into science elective, there's a message on the board.

HAPPY FRIDAY!
RESEARCH TOPICS MUST BE FINALIZED TODAY!

The smiley faces seem to be mocking me. The last few days, my brain has been stuck in a tug-of-war with Ms. Dupart's advice. Maybe she's right, and I should face what I fear. But if I could, I'd run away from this project and never look back.

Hazel, on the other hand, is beaming. Before she even

sets down her backpack, she's already talking about the bees. She's excited, and the words pour out fast. It takes me a minute to understand what she's saying, but after a while, I get it. The next day, she and her mom will drive to Newford to get their bees and move them to Willow Pond.

"How do you move bees?" I ask. I imagine a cloud of bees flying behind a car, but obviously that can't be right.

"Carefully," she answers. It sounds like a joke answer, but her eyes are round and serious. She's wearing the same sweater she had on earlier that day, which seems to have a Greek goddess theme. I think I see one that is supposed to be Athena. Hazel's earrings are large purple owls, which sway as she talks.

"We have to move them at night so we can be sure none are out foraging for pollen and nectar. They'd never find their way back to the hive."

My stomach does a triple flip. I guess I never thought the bees would really be moving to Willow Pond. I was sure Mrs. Bailey would stop them.

"Come to my house Sunday afternoon," she says. "We can work on the first part of our project. And the bees will be there!" Her eyes shine with excitement.

I want to make up an excuse, but I can't think of anything. And we do need to start working on our project.

"I'm sorry they won't be very active," Hazel says.

"Because of the move?" I ask.

"Because it's winter," she says, mouth turning in a frown. "It's nothing like spring, when they'll be flying everywhere, so happy to be around all the flowers."

I try not to shudder. Bees everywhere is not my idea of a good time. But then I remember Ms. Dupart's words about a scientist facing her fears.

I ignore the wave of dizziness that passes through my brain.

"All right," I say. "I'll be there."

When the bell rings, I find Beatrix in the hall. Together, we make our way to her mom's car.

"I can't believe Ms. Dupart is still making you do that project," Beatrix says, sounding annoyed. "Did you really tell her you wanted to do something else?"

I frown. "Yes! I told you I did. She said I couldn't switch."

This might not be true. She said I shouldn't switch. I'm not sure if she said I couldn't. But it's easier to explain *couldn't* to Beatrix.

Beatrix opens the car door and slides across the back seat. "It's your own fault. *You're* the one who picked an elective with homework, bees, *and* the Bee Girl. I bet you're sorry you left dance." She laughs like she's joking and playing around, but it doesn't feel funny.

"Hey, girls," says Mrs. Bailey. "What're you talking about?"

"How Meg is going to get herself stung when she does that bee project," Beatrix says. "Did you know Hazel is moving thousands of bees to our neighborhood?"

I gulp. The idea of getting stung makes me want to throw up. "I hope not." I try to make my voice sound sure, when inside all I can think is how much it would hurt. "Hazel says they won't be very active, not this weekend anyway."

"Hold on." Mrs. Bailey glances at me in the rearview mirror. "Are you saying that Astrid woman is moving bees to Willow Pond?"

I shift in my seat as I fasten my belt. "That's what Hazel said."

Mrs. Bailey pulls away from the curb, frowning. "I wonder if Shirley Johnston knows that bees are going to be kept on her rental property." She drums her fingers on the steering wheel, like she's thinking.

"You could call her," Beatrix says. "You could ask what her little dog, Gloria, thinks about gators and palm trees and then casually mention it."

Mrs. Bailey tips her head to the side. "You think so?"

Beatrix sits up straight. "I think it's your responsibility. You said bees would mess up property values. And we don't want a bunch of bees living in our backyard."

I think about Hazel's excited smile and feel confused. I don't want the bees to come, and having them stay in Newford would solve my problems. So why do I feel bad?

"Hazel says honey bees don't sting very often," I say.

Beatrix rolls her eyes. "Of course she *says* that. It doesn't mean it's true."

I sink back in my seat.

Mrs. Bailey is focused like a laser beam. By the time we reach my driveway, she's found Mrs. Johnston's number and is starting to dial.

I don't want to hear what happens next, so I wave goodbye to Beatrix and hop out of the car.

"Don't worry," says Beatrix. "Mom will take care of everything."

I watch them pull away. Mrs. Bailey taking care of everything is exactly what I'm afraid of.

CHAPTER

15

Inside, the house is quiet. Mom's at work, Elsie's at Grandma Lou's, and Conrad has band practice for tonight's basketball game at the high school. But I know Dad's upstairs working, because his car is in the driveway.

I dig around until I discover an apple and half a bag of barbecue potato chips. I cut the apple into slices and dump the chips in a bowl. Then I climb the stairs to Dad's office in the attic.

When I peek in, he looks up and grins. Dad says he's too big for a regular desk, so he works at two giant folding tables that have been pushed together. He says this is better for playing board games anyway, which he sometimes needs to do when he's designing them. Plus, it helps hold his mess, which currently consists of sticky notes, sketches, pages of diagrams, and handfuls of little plastic tiles.

"Hey," I say.

Dad looks at the clock. "Oh, hey! Didn't realize it was getting so late. Help me remember to pick up Elsie. Your grandma wouldn't let me hear the end of it."

"I won't," I say, smiling. We're all used to Dad getting lost in the creative process.

"I'm at a frustrating part, actually." He eyes my snack. "I assume you brought that to share."

I crunch a chip. "Nope."

Dad sighs. "The only thing I don't like about my office is how far away it is from the kitchen."

I don't feel bad for him. I've seen the epic sandwiches he makes for lunch.

He sighs and runs his fingers through his hair, which makes it stand up on end.

He looks at me hopefully. "Will you do a play test with me? I need a few rounds to help me think something through."

A game designer has to test games before they're finished. Sometimes Dad needs to see how the game works in order to think through a problem or to see an example of how the players would interact. Play testing can be slow because Dad has to stop and write notes as we play. I don't mind, though. I like seeing what he's working on.

"Sure," I say.

"Great," says Dad. "Get us two other players, and I'll get everything organized."

I sort through the bin of old stuffed animals. Ideally, Dad would want to see the game played with four people. But since there are only two of us, we need a couple of "pretend" players. We will take turns playing their hands.

I select Edward, the frayed walrus that used to belong to Conrad. Then I dig around for Toast, a wonky-eyed bat that I named when I was three. The game board is sketched out on a few pieces of taped-together paper, so I arrange Edward and Toast on opposite sides.

Dad explains the game while he deals the cards. The idea is that there is one goal that the players are supposed to achieve. But in addition, each player is given a secret task to complete that gives points. The task could either help or hurt the chances of the group achieving the goal.

The first round we play is super slow. Dad mutters under his breath a lot and scribbles with his pencil. Toast is leaning to the side, so I fix him the best I can. His eyes are sideways, but he can't help it.

We play another two rounds. It isn't quite at the level of being fun yet, but I can see the idea has potential.

Halfway through the fourth game, Dad checks the clock again. "Let's stop here so I can write down a few notes and then go get your sister."

"Who do you think would have won?" I ask.

Dad taps his pencil against the table. "Good question. Edward's hand is strong, but I think Toast might have turned things around."

I laugh. Being with him in his office is fun. Elsie isn't here to destroy the pieces, and Conrad isn't around to point out everything Dad should do differently. And no matter how sticky a game problem is, I can always walk away.

"And what about me? You don't think I might have won?" I'd been behind, but stranger things have happened— especially when a game is in its testing phase.

Dad smiles. "The smart money's on you, that's for sure."

"What's this one called anyway?" I ask.

"Not sure." Dad sighs. "Maybe Evildoer? Because of the sabotage stuff?"

I think it over. "It's catchy."

"The company I'm working with likes it," Dad says. "But something about it doesn't sit right with me. I don't know if anyone, even super-bad dudes, thinks of themselves that way. Because in real life, everyone is the hero of their own story. You know?"

"Dad?" I grin. "You *may* be overthinking."

Dad laughs. "Maybe you're right. What's a little evildoing among friends anyhow? A teensy bit of sabotage?"

He says the word "sabotage" in a terrible French accent, twirling an imaginary mustache. Even though I laugh, the word makes me think about Mrs. Bailey and the bees. Mrs. Bailey is trying to sabotage Hazel and Astrid, and they don't even know it.

"Dad, did you know that new girl Hazel and her mom are beekeepers?"

"I didn't know," says Dad. "That's kind of cool."

"Mrs. Bailey does *not* think they are cool," I say. "She said something about trying to stop them because they're renting their house. Could Mrs. Johnston do that?"

Dad wrinkles his forehead in a V, thinking. "Mrs. Johnston is her landlord, so she probably has a say in how the property is used. I can't imagine the bees would damage the property. But it's probably up to Mrs. Johnston."

"We need the bees for our project," I say. "Ms. Dupart says no switching."

"She'd probably understand if something happened to the bees," he says.

If the bees go away, Hazel might let us pick a non-biting, non-stinging insect. I should feel happy about that.

Dad grabs the snack bowl, scooping up a handful of chips and a couple of apple slices and tossing them into his wide-open mouth.

"Hey, no stealing!" I'm not hungry anymore, but I can't let that go without a fight.

Dad scoots the bowl back across the table to me. He munches thoughtfully. "How do you think Hazel would feel about switching from bees?"

I think about Hazel. She likes bees—maybe even *loves* them. I look at Dad, chomping the last few chips.

"Sad, I guess. Maybe mad," I say finally. The words don't seem strong enough.

"Hmm," says Dad.

I remember Hazel's bee socks, how people stared and whispered. "But her life might be easier if she didn't love bees so much."

I think of Mrs. Bailey, making her phone call about the bees. Mrs. Bailey trying to get Hazel removed from science elective. Hazel has been here only a short time, but she already has someone who doesn't like her. A powerful someone.

"We can't always help what we love," Dad says quietly, almost to himself.

I look at him, surprised, but he's already gone back to his notes.

CHAPTER

16

On Sunday afternoon, I walk to Hazel's house. I start to get nervous, and then I realize why. This is the first time in ages that I've gone to the house of someone new. I'm not sure what to expect.

I chew my thumb as I turn onto Maple Way. Hazel's street is on the opposite side of the hill from Beatrix's house on Poplar. The houses on Maple Way are small and close together, with brightly painted front doors. The street has a friendly feel, with houses nestled against the curve of the hill.

Hazel's house is pale green, and the door is cherry red—not the color of candy but the deep red of cherries from the expensive grocery store. In the front yard, there's a maple tree that lost its leaves months ago. When I tilt my head, I can look up through the bare branches until I see Beatrix's house at the top of the hill. Beatrix is out of town this weekend for a dance event, but if she were at her window, she could see me looking up.

Three steps take me to the porch, which has a swing with peeling paint. A moment after I knock, Hazel comes to the door.

"Hi!" she says. Today her sweater has a vegetable theme. I see beets, carrots, and lettuce. She's holding a potato masher in one hand.

I follow her through the living room, past a squishy-looking couch. I don't see Astrid anywhere. The room is stacked with moving boxes. A few are open and seem like they've been rummaged through.

"Hazel," I say. "Why are you holding a potato masher?"

"Oh!" Hazel looks like she forgot she was holding it. "I was looking for a spatula."

I peer at the boxes. "Did you find one?"

She shakes her head. "We aren't the most organized packers. I found a big spoon, though, so that should work. I might make cookies later." She hesitates, tugging at the sleeve of her sweater. "Or I could make them now."

I pause.

"Only if you want to," she says quickly. "You don't have to. But maybe it would be fun? And everyone likes cookies, right?"

The words tumble out in a rush.

I'm unsure. But when I look into her hopeful, excited face, there's no way I can say no.

"Yeah," I say. "Cookies sound good."

She grins.

"Where's the recipe?"

She frowns thoughtfully. "I'm pretty sure we are okay without one. I've made cookies lots of times. We may need to substitute a few things, though."

Before I can answer, she's poking her head into a cabinet.

"Great. We don't have flour, but we can use oatmeal instead. That should work, right?"

My insides sink a bit. I always feel better with a plan.

"Come on," she says. "Go ahead and poke around, and we'll see what we can find."

Together we look in every box, cabinet, and drawer. Astrid and Hazel's packing method *was* completely disorganized. In one box, I find a cheese grater, a hairbrush, a box of screws, and a miniature oil painting. But there's something kind of fun and mysterious about the jumbled-up stuff, like I don't know what I'm going to find each time I tear open a box.

"How about this?" I say, holding up a half-full container of rainbow sprinkles.

"Oh, definitely," Hazel answers. She adds a jar of applesauce to the pile.

After we have looked through everything, we examine the potential ingredients.

"Not bad," Hazel says, checking the vanilla. "Although I can't believe we moved this from Newford when there're only about two drops left."

Through some kind of miracle, we've also found butter, eggs, and baking powder.

"We don't have sugar but have lots of honey," says Hazel.

"And the sprinkles," I add.

"Of course!" She grins. "How could I forget?"

I look at the ingredients. Without a recipe, I don't know where to start. We don't know how much to add, or the order to do it in. These cookies will be a disaster.

Hazel adds butter to a bowl and mashes it. She sees my face. "Think of it as an experiment. Do you want to add the oatmeal?"

I hesitate. "I don't know how much to add."

Hazel shrugs. "Whatever you think looks right. If the batter looks too wet, we'll just add some more oatmeal at the end."

"What if I mess it up?" I ask.

"Look," Hazel says. "It's not a big deal. We're starting with things that taste good before they are baked, so they should taste pretty good after. Probably even better. If not, we can always start over."

I chew the inside of my lip, thinking. "I'm not sure. What if they're bad?"

Hazel rolls her eyes but not in a mean way. "Have you ever had a *bad* cookie?"

She looks at me expectantly, smiling widely.

"Okay," I say finally. "I guess either way, it's better than no cookies at all."

Hazel laughs, and I feel myself grin back. I realize that she doesn't mind it if the cookies don't turn out. Maybe she thinks it's part of the fun.

We work together to mix the ingredients. I pour in the oatmeal and accidentally add too much. But, like Hazel said, we add extra egg and applesauce to make it stick together.

When it's time to add the honey, she pours some onto a spoon and hands it to me.

"Try it," she says.

I'm expecting it to be sugary sweet, like normal honey. But it's different—there's so much more there. The flavors are somehow layered on top of one another, like flowers and sunshine all mixed together. If summer had a taste, this would be it.

She watches my face and grins. "More?"

I hold out my spoon. It's just as amazing as before.

"This is delicious, Hazel," I say. "If people knew how good this was, they would never eat regular honey again. This is from your bees?"

Hazel's smile is full of pride. "Yep. Glad you like it."

It's cozy in the kitchen, with the sun coming through

the window. The dough is stiff, so we take turns stirring. Then we taste-test.

"Not bad," I say.

Hazel looks thoughtful. "It needs more pizzazz."

I smile at the word, which reminds me of Grandma Lou. But she's right. It could use a little something extra.

"Maybe chocolate chips?" I ask. "Or a chocolate bar that we could chop up?"

She frowns for a moment, then brightens. "No chocolate. But we do have oranges. We could squeeze them and add the juice."

I shake my head. "Juice will make them too watery. It will mess up our ratio."

She looks disappointed. I am, too, for a minute. But then I remember, snapping my fingers.

"We'll use the zest instead," I say. "That's what my dad does when he makes his lemon waffles."

I show her how to cut the bitter white part away from the peel. Then we chop it into tiny pieces and sprinkle them in.

"All the flavor, without making the dough wet," I say.

"Smart," she says, sounding impressed. "That was a good idea."

I'm grinning. I like that she took my idea seriously. And the orange pieces make the whole kitchen smell brighter somehow.

This time when we sample the dough, it tastes just right. We scoop the cookies onto the sheet.

Hazel prods one. "They're a bit lumpy. Maybe they will smooth out as they bake."

I give her a light shove on the arm. "Ha! What happened to *cookies are cookies; it's impossible to mess them up?*"

For some reason, this makes Hazel bust up laughing.

I'm laughing, too. I wave my spoon in the air. "I knew you weren't super laid-back about everything!"

Hazel wipes her eyes. "You were *so* serious about it! Like if we didn't make the most perfect cookies, the universe might implode!"

"But maybe it will, Hazel! Maybe it will," I say.

We lean against the counter, still cracking up. My worries from before are a million miles away. Who could ever want perfect cookies when making them this way is so much fun?

We slide the trays into the oven and then fill their dishwasher. Soon, the kitchen is quiet except for the sound of the dishwasher sloshing.

Hazel puts a teakettle on the stove. As the cookies bake, the smells of oranges and honey fill the kitchen.

"So, where's your mom?" I ask. "Is she working or something?"

"She went to a craft fair in Blakely," Hazel says. Blakely is two towns over. "She sells her handmade jewelry there."

I remember the necklace Astrid wore at the party. "She's a jewelry designer?"

The teakettle whistles, and Hazel goes to it. "Not as a

job—more of a hobby. She makes some money from it, but most of it goes back into buying more supplies. She works for Babbage's."

Babbage's Market is the fancy grocery store. It has wood floors, and they play classical music. Dad loves to buy cheese there, even though Mom can't stand how expensive it is. She tells him to remove the stickers before he brings it home so she can enjoy it without thinking about the price.

Hazel kind of half laughs to herself. "It's sort of funny we don't have more food here, isn't it? But she doesn't usually work at the stores unless she's doing training or they're opening a new one. She works in their main office."

She adds a tea bag to each mug and pours the hot water over them.

The kitchen table is covered with photographs, snapshots of Hazel and Astrid doing nature stuff: climbing Pilot Mountain, standing on a swing bridge, wearing headlamps inside a cave. I think about her dad and his deepsea research. Maybe all the members of Hazel's family like adventures.

"That was interesting about your dad and the submarine," I say.

She looks at me with an expression I can't read.

"About the octopus," I say. "The seven-armed one that really has eight."

"Oh, right," Hazel says.

"I would love to do research on a submarine someday," I say. "Although that is sad that you basically can't talk to your family for months. No calls in or out, right?"

Hazel doesn't answer. The corners of her mouth turn down a bit. My stomach twists. I don't know what I was thinking, asking her about her dad. Of course she misses him while he's away. I hate it when my mom is away on work trips, and those don't last for months at a time. I try to think of a way to change the subject, a way to get us back to the easy laughter from before. When the timer finally dings, I sigh in relief.

Hazel pops out of her chair, like she's glad for the interruption. She looks over her shoulder at me. "Don't you want to help me check to see if they're done?"

She's not mad at me. I grin until it stretches my cheeks. "Of course!"

Hazel finds oven mitts and opens the oven door. When she does, a blast of oatmeal-orange-honey goodness hits me, and I want to gobble up the cookies immediately. They are a beautiful shade of brown.

I use a butter knife to help move them from the cookie sheet to a plate. They're soft, and a few crumble a bit, but it's not a big deal. Hazel doesn't even blink.

We aren't patient enough to let them cool. They are a little sticky with the honey. But they are crispy and delicious.

"Yum," I say. I already know I want another.

Hazel is still chewing her cookie. Her forehead is scrunched in concentration. Finally, she speaks. "Mm! The orange zest makes them perfect."

I look at the cookies. Really, they aren't perfect at all. The oven didn't transform them. They're still lumpy and shaped weird. The applesauce might not match the other flavors. But for some reason, sitting here in Hazel's kitchen, imperfect feels okay. Maybe *imperfect* is exactly what I need.

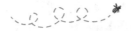

By the time we get another batch in and out of the oven, we've each eaten six cookies and refilled our mugs for a second round of tea.

"I guess we should start thinking about our project," Hazel says. She disappears and then returns, carrying a stack of bee books. She piles them on the table and then sits down.

I pick up one called *Bees & Wasps: A Compendium.* I flip the book open and come face-to-face with a monster. The body is black and shiny, and it looks like it would love to bite me in two. I can't stop staring.

"This thing is a nightmare," I say. "I can't believe you like them."

Hazel looks at the page, frowning. "That's a wasp, not a bee." She reaches across the table and flips to a different section. "See, the honey bee is fuzzy and cute."

I look down at the page. Only Hazel could describe a

bee as cute. But I will admit that bees look nicer than wasps. Still, that's not saying much.

We sit at the table, quiet. I curl my fingers around my tea mug, which is warm but not hot. I help myself to another cookie.

"By the way, you're a good baker," Hazel says.

"Thanks," I say, smiling. "You are, too."

This feels really comfortable, like we've known each other for years. I can't believe this is my first time at Hazel's house.

She points out the window. At first, I can't tell what she's pointing at, but then I see something about the size of a file box.

"That's the beehive," Hazel says. "We moved it last night."

I can't help it—a smile spreads across my face until it almost reaches my ears. I thought Mrs. Bailey was unstoppable, but somehow Hazel did it! Mrs. Bailey wasn't able to block the bees after all. I look around the room, with its half-opened boxes and the cookie crumbs we left, and I realize two things. The first is that I like it here. And the second is that I haven't thought about Beatrix all afternoon. I haven't been worried about saying the wrong thing or doing the wrong thing. I haven't wondered about someone freezing me out. Being with Hazel has been nice. Fun, even. A lot more than I expected. The thought makes my smile even bigger.

A few bees circle the hive. "Will they be confused, now that they aren't in Newford?"

"With bees, there's a saying. You can move them less than three feet and they are okay," Hazel says. "Or you can move them more than three *miles* and they are okay. Anything in between, they do get confused."

I think about it for a moment. "Almost like a big move makes their brains reset, and they know they are somewhere different."

"Yeah," says Hazel. There's a bitter edge to her voice. "They're lucky."

I swallow my bite of cookie and wipe my mouth. I'm not sure what to say.

Hazel pushes her mug to the side. "I wish I could do a reset on my brain, too."

She's looking out the window, and it's hard to read her expression.

"You don't like it here?" I ask.

Hazel shrugs. "I thought small towns were supposed to be friendly, but everyone here already knows each other. Since birth, practically. So I stick out. Supposedly Willow Pond is stronger academically, but they still had to skip me up two grades for math. I do my class on a computer with a high school teacher."

I frown. I didn't realize that she had been skipped up so far in math. "So where do you go during math block?"

"Ms. Fisher's class, but she never even talks to me,

even during science time. But honestly, she's so mean it's probably better this way."

Ms. Fisher is the kind of teacher all the kids tell stories about, but I've never had her. "Too bad you don't have Ms. Dupart."

Hazel nods slowly, but she's biting her lip, and her eyes are turned down. She looks like she might cry. I need to think of something helpful to say.

"It's your first week here," I say. "Willow Pond is a big change from Newford, so maybe you're still adjusting. You lived in Newford a long time, and had all those different clubs. Starting over is hard."

"I do miss Newford," Hazel admits. "Claudia is there, my friend who is a beekeeper." She says "Claudia" like the word "cloud" plus "ee-uh," which I think is Spanish.

"When you walk around, there's always a crowd," Hazel continues. "No one looks at you, as long as you don't block the sidewalk. No one sticks out. Here it seems like there's less stuff for people to do. Everyone is in each other's business more."

"Maybe," I say. "But that's not bad. It will be okay after you make friends. A small town means people look out for their neighbors."

Hazel shrugs. "I don't know about that. Someone called our landlord to try to stop us from moving the bees."

My heart shrinks up. It was Mrs. Bailey, of course. I look down at my mug.

"Wow," I say. "Did they tell you who complained?"

"Mrs. Johnston didn't say," Hazel continues. "She said she doesn't mind about the bees, but if it causes trouble with the neighborhood, we'll have to talk again."

"Lots of people don't like bees," I say. "People are probably afraid of getting stung."

Hazel traces a stain on the wood table. "We need bees, even if someone dislikes them. There's a bunch of food that wouldn't grow without bees pollinating it. Bees are dying off, and it's our job to help them."

"And allergies," I say, feeling braver. "Some people are allergic."

"Allergies, yeah," Hazel admits. "But the thing is, honey bees don't want to hurt people. All they want to do is collect nectar and pollen. If a bee stings someone, she dies. Stinging is never a first choice."

Maybe Hazel has a point. Being afraid isn't enough. But at the same time, it's hard to squash down my fear. Whenever I think about bees, I get hit by a wave of dizziness. It's not just about the stinging; it's also the idea of them crawling over one another inside the dark hive. But when I look at Hazel's face, I can see how much she loves the bees. And if bees are important to the Earth, maybe they should be given a chance.

We flip through the books for a while, but after a few minutes of reading, we decide it's time for another cookie break.

Hazel points at me with a half-eaten cookie. "If you were a marsupial, which one would you be?"

"That's easy: koala. What about you?"

"Quokka," says Hazel, as if it's obvious. "They're in the same family as kangaroos and wallabies, but they're little, like the size of a cat."

We pause so I can look them up. They are weirdly cute.

"Lemon or lime?" I ask.

"Limes for sure," says Hazel. "They're more zippy. You?"

"Lemons," I say. "Limes are too sour. Favorite subject?"

"Back home, science," she says. "Here it's science elective, so far, I think."

"Me too," I say.

We go back and forth like that for a while. Turns out, we have other things in common besides our love for science and our baking skills. It's not that our answers match up; it's that she finds these questions fun to talk about, too.

I hear a car in the driveway. It must be Hazel's mom. I look at the time—it's almost five o'clock.

"I better go," I say. "My parents told me to be home for dinner."

"Do you want to take some cookies with you?" Hazel asks.

"Sure," I say.

She finds a paper plate and stacks it with cookies. "Here's enough for your family, and a couple extra so you can have some on the way home."

I smile. "That's really nice, Hazel. Thanks."

She smiles back. "Maybe you could come over again sometime soon. Next Sunday?"

"Sure," I say. "We've got a lot to do on that project."

"The project." She nods. "Right. Maybe we should get together every Sunday."

We walk into the front yard together. Astrid is getting out of a little red car. Her smile widens when she sees that I'm still at their house.

"Hey there," she says. "How was the project?"

Hazel grins. "It was good. We made cookies."

"Yum," says Astrid. She opens the hatchback of her car. There are lots of boxes inside.

Hazel takes one and carries it up to the house. "'Bye, Meg! See you tomorrow!"

I pause. "Do you want me to help?"

"No, that's all right," Astrid says. "But listen, Meg, I need to ask you something. How does Hazel seem to you?"

Astrid is watching me closely. I want to tell her that I barely know Hazel. I might not be the best person to say how she's doing.

"Okay, I guess—she misses Newford," I say finally. Then I think back to how sad she seemed when we talked earlier this afternoon. "I think she misses her dad. How he can't call or write from where he is. It must be hard."

Astrid frowns. "Her dad doesn't come around very often, but that isn't anything new."

I nod. "Right, because of the submarine."

Astrid doesn't seem to hear me. "It about broke her heart when he took that teaching job in Ohio. Not that she ever saw him that much, but at least she knew he was nearby. I thought this move might help. We needed a change of scenery, too."

Hazel comes back before I can respond. Astrid gives me a little nod, and they both say goodbye.

The whole way home, I think about Astrid's words. *Teaching job? Ohio?* I don't know exactly what happened back there, but I do know one thing: there are no submarine research expeditions in Ohio. No seven-armed octopuses, either.

ANIMAL FIELDWORK PROJECT

MS. DUPART

EXPLORATORY SCIENCE

SECOND SEMESTER

SIXTH PERIOD

PART

3

Describe a defense mechanism your subject might use.

30 points

Honey bees use their stingers to defend themselves. The honey bee stinger is barbed, which means it has a pointy bit at the end. If the bee stings another animal, the barb makes the stinger stay behind in the other animal's skin. The venom keeps pumping the whole time the stinger is embedded. A worker bee can use her stinger once. If she uses it, she dies.

A queen bee has a smooth stinger. Mostly, she uses it to help her lay eggs, but sometimes she uses it to fight. If two queens hatch at once, they will fight to the death. Because the stinger is smooth, she can sting again and again. Usually the queen uses her stinger only when she is fighting for dominance.

CHAPTER

17

Tuesday morning, at the end of literacy block, Mr. Thornton calls up Hazel to the front of the class. She's wearing a black sweater with yellow hexagons all over it—a honeycomb pattern. She's holding a paper bag and is grinning widely. Uh-oh. I don't have a good feeling about this.

"Everyone, listen up. We've got a special treat today." Mr. Thornton speaks in that way teachers have when they want you to get excited about something. "Go ahead, Hazel."

Hazel removes a jar of honey and a stack of wooden craft sticks from the paper bag.

"I thought you guys might want to try the honey from my bees," she says. "Meg tried it at my house last weekend and said it was delicious."

Twenty-eight sets of eyes swivel to look at me. I sink low in my seat.

Beatrix's stare zaps me like an electrical current. I gulp.

"Right, Meg?" Hazel says. "You really liked it, right?"

My face is burning. "It's good."

"Who wants to try?" Hazel looks like she's expecting everyone's hands to launch into the air, desperate to be the first. No one moves.

Finally, Beatrix raises her hand. Hazel brightens, ready to hand her a sample.

"I have a question," says Beatrix. "Isn't honey basically bee barf?"

"Barf?" Hazel is puzzled.

"You know." Beatrix nods: "Throw-up. Vomit. Puke."

"Eww!" at least half the class says. The other half giggles.

"My honey's not made of vomit," says Hazel quickly.

"Wait. That's a good question, actually," says Tyler from the third row. "Where does honey come from? Is it from bee butts?"

Everyone cracks up at this except Hazel, Mr. Thornton, and me.

"Bee diarrhea," Ryan adds.

"All right, people," says Mr. Thornton.

Hazel is blushing hotly, but she tries to explain. "Bees make honey in their honey stomachs. And then, yes, it comes out of their mouths. But it's not throw-up. And it's definitely not diarrhea."

Mr. Thornton seems to realize this is not going well. "I'm happy to try some."

Hazel hands him a sample, and he tastes it.

"Very good," he says. "Would anyone else like to try?"

The room is quiet. Finally, Ryan stands up.

"I will," says Ryan. "I love bee puke."

He takes the sample and makes a throw-up sound. Everyone cracks up. Even in a room full of laughter, I can pick out Beatrix's giggle.

Hazel's shoulders slump as she looks at the floor. I can't stand it.

I want to tell everyone that they're being ridiculous. Humans have eaten honey for thousands of years. I open my mouth and try to make the words come out, but they stick in my throat. My heart is beating so fast. I lean over my desk with my head between my hands. I focus on my breath going in and out. It helps when I get nervous.

"I can't believe you ate the bee-butt honey," Beatrix mutters.

"It's just normal honey," I whisper back. "It's actually good."

Beatrix tosses her hair and turns to Zoe.

When the bell rings, Hazel grabs her backpack and runs out the door. Left behind on the table is the jar of honey nobody wants.

In the lunchroom, I find myself checking for Hazel. She's at her regular table with Cora, who now has a purple streak in her hair that matches her glasses. Hazel seems okay, and when I realize that, it feels like a weight lifts off me. Hazel is more than okay—she's smiling and talking with Cora. I'm surprised to feel a pull inside, like I want to join them. I wonder what it would be like to have lunch at a different table.

Beatrix taps my arm. Her forehead is wrinkled in concern. "Are you feeling all right?"

I look at her, confused. "I'm fine. Why do you ask?"

Beatrix smiles sweetly. "I mean, after eating bee puke last weekend."

Oh. She's back to making fun of the honey. "Come on, Beatrix. It's just regular honey."

Beatrix's smile turns into a scowl. "Why are you sticking up for her? And why were you even at her house?"

"We have a project to work on, remember?" I say. "She's actually okay, Beatrix. She's nice."

But this seems to make Beatrix more upset. "She's *not* okay. She acts like she's better than us. Why does Mr. Thornton let her have class time for honey samples? And why does he let her talk on and on about things anyway? Who cares if she can compare the book we're reading to some Shakespeare book she read at her school in Newford?"

Arshi picks at a stray piece of lint on her basketball hoodie. "*Plays.* Shakespeare wrote plays, not books."

Beatrix scowls. "Whatever, Arshi! The point is that she talks too much. It's like she thinks her opinions are as important as Mr. Thornton's, when he is the teacher."

Hazel, on the other side of the lunchroom, laughs at something Cora says. Now I wish even more that I could join them.

"And," Beatrix says, her voice rising, "I can't believe they actually moved bees into our neighborhood. Fifty thousand of them."

This gets the whole table's attention.

Zoe opens a package of pretzels with a *pop*. "She did? I thought your mom was going to stop that."

"She tried to," Beatrix says. "But Mrs. Johnston said it wasn't a big deal. Not a big deal for her, maybe. She's all the way down in Florida! Not next door to a million bees."

"Maybe it's not such a big deal," I say. "The bees haven't bothered anyone. Hazel says they aren't aggressive."

I'm peeling my orange, and it makes me think of the zest in the cookies at Hazel's. When I look up, I realize that all the girls are looking at me. Especially Beatrix, who has her arms crossed and a nasty look on her face.

"Seriously, Meg? You're going to choose her side in this?" Beatrix's voice cracks, like she's really upset.

I'm so confused. First Beatrix is mad that I went over there to work on a school project. And now, just because I say the bees might be okay, she sounds like she's going to cry.

"I'm not picking a side," I say, putting down my orange.

Beatrix shakes her head. "Ever since she got here, you have been acting so weird. Maybe you'd rather be sitting with her. Go ahead—go sit with her."

The table becomes still and quiet, but the *boom-boom* of my heartbeat is somehow trying to make up for it. I feel sick. Even though I think it might be fun to sit with Hazel and Cora, I don't want to do it like this. This feels like a challenge. If I leave the table now, I don't think they'll ever want me back. Beatrix-and-Meg will be gone forever. I'm not ready for that.

"I want to be here with you guys," I say. "Don't do this."

No one moves except Zoe, who chews her pretzels and looks back and forth at Beatrix and me.

"Okay," says Beatrix. "I get it. You're doing a school project with her. But you better work fast, because those bees have got to go."

The bell rings, and for once, I'm glad lunch is over. We all stand up and head for PE. I'll try to talk to Beatrix later. Sometimes she's different when it's just the two of us.

In science elective, we're supposed to read through the fieldwork research packets. The pages are very detailed, with areas for anatomy and structure, research, observations, and fieldwork. I am not looking forward to the bee observations, but maybe Hazel will cover that part.

The very last page says, *Presentation—details to come.*

"What do you think this means?" I ask Hazel.

"I don't think she's covered it yet," Hazel says. "Maybe a report about our data?"

I puff out my cheeks in a sigh. "Let's start with the first part. 'Anatomy: draw a detailed sketch of the animal you are studying. Include details and label parts.'"

Hazel pulls a bee book from her backpack. "Queen bees, workers, and drones are all different. I guess we can pick one to draw."

She opens the book to an illustration that shows three bees in a row, smallest to largest. Tiny hairs cover the bees' striped bodies, all the way down their long segmented legs.

I study them one by one.

The worker bee is an ordinary, basic bee. All workers are female.

Next is the drone—a male—who has giant, cartoonish eyes and looks almost muscular.

The queen bee is biggest. Her abdomen is slightly more pointed than the worker's and drone's.

Hazel taps her pencil on the table, waiting for me to answer.

"Not the drones," I decide. Their only job is to mate with a queen. Every fall, the workers force the drones out so they don't consume precious honey over the long, cold winter.

"We should draw the worker," says Hazel firmly.

"There are thousands of workers, and they do all the important jobs."

I frown. "I don't think they do *all* the important jobs. And she's the *queen*, remember. She's in charge."

"She's not in charge," Hazel answers quickly. "People think that because of the word 'queen,' but in reality, all the bees work together."

"But—" I say.

"Remember," Hazel says. "I've been learning about bees for years, so I know more than you do. We should draw the worker."

My cheeks flush. Hazel takes out a set of colored pencils and starts to sketch a worker.

"Hey," I say, and it comes out like a squeak. I clear my throat. "*Hey.*"

Hazel looks up, blinking.

"You don't get to choose," I say. "We have to decide together. I may not know as much about bees as you, but this class is really important to me. You don't get to pick what we're going to do."

Hazel's mouth drops open. She shuts it again.

"And," I say, "if you know so much about bees, you should slow down a little and actually try to help me understand. It doesn't help me learn if you just tell me what to do."

She doesn't say anything.

I bite the skin on the side of my thumb. *That's it. This*

project is going to be a disaster. She's going to be mad at me,
and we're stuck together the entire semester.

Hazel puts her pencil down. "What do you want to know?"

She doesn't even seem mad. I'm shocked, but I recover. "What do you mean, the queen isn't in charge? She is the queen. Isn't that what it means?"

Hazel's eyes light up. "Actually, a better way to think of a colony is as a *superorganism.*"

I frown. I know "organism" means an individual animal or plant. But I don't know what a superorganism is.

"It's like this," Hazel says, flipping over her paper. She draws a stick figure of a person.

"Let's call this guy 'Bob,'" Hazel says. She writes his name on the paper. I'm not sure what this has to do with bees, but I watch her draw.

"So Bob has cells and organs, and they all do special jobs. Like, his stomach digests food. His lungs take in oxygen. Okay?"

I study her drawing. "Don't forget his brain."

"Yeah, you're right. The nervous system." Hazel draws a squiggle in Bob's head. Then, next to Bob, she draws a beehive. She draws little dots inside the beehive. I guess they represent the bees.

"You could look at these bees as individual organisms. I mean, they *are,* technically. Or you could think of them organized by the jobs they do, like preparing or distributing food, regulating the temperature of the hive, clean-up, security."

The idea of it slowly starts to come together for me. Bees do their jobs as individuals. But looking at the colony together, it adds up almost to what one living being would do. All the individuals come together to make one big superorganism.

"That's pretty cool," I say. "So you're saying they all work together. They're all equally important. Even the drones."

Hazel taps her pencil. "I was thinking the workers are more important because of all the work they do, but you're right. They're all important."

"Still," I say. "Even if they're important, the queen is *necessary*. Without her, there literally wouldn't be any new workers."

We're quiet for a moment, thinking.

"We need to draw them all," I say finally. It's more work, but when I think of them as a superorganism, they should all be represented.

"I think you're right," says Hazel. "Is it okay if I draw the worker?"

I nod. I sketch an outline of the queen's round head and her oddly pointed body.

We don't talk much after that. Our pencils *scritch-scratch* as we draw. At one point, she asks me if I think she should make the antennae longer. A few minutes later, I ask

144

how she drew the wings to make them look transparent.
We work until the bell rings. It's quiet, but nobody's mad.

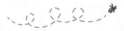

It's Tuesday afternoon, so I meet Beatrix at our corner.
The afternoon is warm, so we run a bit with Bart and Lola.

We talk about normal stuff for our first lap around the
soccer field. It feels like what happened at lunch is forgot-
ten. But on our second lap, she clears her throat, like she
has something to say.

"I know you think I was too harsh earlier," Beatrix says.

I want to say "Yeah, obviously"—but if I do that, Beatrix will stop talking. I want to understand what she's
thinking.

So instead, I shrug. "Why does she bug you so much?"

She rolls her eyes. "Besides the fact that she's annoying
and weird?"

I sigh. *Beatrix.*

"Okay, okay." Beatrix straightens her ponytail. "It's
sort of your fault. I'm *still* kind of mad that you aren't
doing dance." She makes a sound that's almost like laughing, but her eyes are serious.

"I know you're mad," I say. "What should I do? I have
to be partners with her."

"When Hazel came, everything changed," Beatrix
says. "And you hung out with her on the weekend, too.
I don't get it."

"For our project," I remind her again. "And she's not so bad. She's nice, actually."

When I look at Beatrix, her eyes are watering. She wipes at them quickly, like she doesn't want me to see.

My eyes widen. "What's wrong? Are you crying?"

"I'm not," she says, sniffling.

I grab her in a hug, and she hugs me back. It's that normal Beatrix-and-Meg feeling. But after a few seconds, she pulls away.

"Stress," she says. "Lots going on right now with dance."

I frown. Dance is Beatrix's favorite thing. It's not supposed to be stressful.

"Wait a second," I say. "What's going on with dance?"

Beatrix scrubs at her eyes again, like she's trying to push the tears back into her eyeballs.

"I want to start doing more contemporary work but Mom says it's not worth it, that it will destroy my focus. It doesn't matter to her that sometimes I hate ballet."

I'm shocked. Beatrix's whole life plan is to be a ballerina, and now she's saying she doesn't even like it anymore.

"Maybe you can take a break," I say.

"No way," says Beatrix tightly. "Taking a break at my age, at my stage, is impossible. My mom would never let that happen."

Mrs. Bailey is serious about Beatrix and dance. I'm not sure what to say.

"She wants you to be happy," I say. "You've put in so much work."

She waves her hand like she's pushing all her feelings away. "Don't worry about me. It doesn't matter." Her voice sounds sharp and angry.

I touch her arm. "Come on, Beatrix. Of course it matters."

She pulls away quickly. "It sounds like Hazel is basically your new best friend, so you're all set."

She seems so angry. I don't understand it.

I shake my head. "Don't say that."

"Are you sure?" Beatrix asks. "Because it sounds to me like Hazel is perfect. Perfect science brain. Perfect friend. Perfect stupid bees."

"She isn't perfect," I say.

Beatrix shrugs, like she doesn't believe me.

"She *isn't*," I say again, but Beatrix won't look at me. I'm trying to break through her shell, but I can't. I want her to know that Hazel isn't taking her place, could never take her place.

I sigh. "You know how she told us her dad was in the ocean on a submarine, looking for that octopus? Well, Astrid said he is actually a teacher in Ohio."

Beatrix looks at me now, her eyebrows drawn together. "That doesn't make sense."

"Okay?" I say. "It doesn't matter, though. The point is that no one is perfect. Not me, not you, not Hazel."

"Still best friends?" Beatrix is smiling, but her voice shakes a bit.

I'm not always sure about Beatrix. Sometimes I don't like her very much. But no matter what, I love her.

"Still best friends," I repeat.

We grin at each other.

It feels like the bad stuff has been washed away. She tells me that Knox will be home from college soon, and the whole family is going to the beach, even the dogs. She seems happy when she talks about the trip. The water will be too cold for swimming, but she doesn't mind.

Our friendship may have some broken-down parts, but I'm not going to throw it away like it's nothing. It's true that Beatrix was mean to Hazel today, but she's more than that. She's sleepovers and s'mores, patty-cake with Elsie, and trips to the warm green ocean at Gingerbread Island. She's seven whole years of birthday cakes, playing with puppies, and sledding down Turner Hill.

A best friend is not a single thing. A best friend is the key to an entire universe.

We hold on to Bart and Lola and run all the way home.

CHAPTER
18

It's Sunday afternoon, and that means Hazel and I are working on our project. Today will be different because Hazel is going to examine the hive while I'm here. She'll open the whole thing so she can check each frame. Today, everything she wears has stripes. It's like she picked her clothes in honor of the occasion. I'm getting used to her unusual combinations, even if they hurt my eyes sometimes.

"Are you sure you don't want to suit up?" Hazel asks. "You could wear my mom's gear."

I shake my head. There's no way I ever want to look inside the hive. I've tried to tell Hazel that I'm afraid, but she doesn't really understand. Plus, I don't want to talk about fainting when I get nervous. She's the only kid in town who doesn't know, and I'd like to keep it that way.

Hazel sighs, like I don't know what I'm missing. "The bee suit would keep you safe. It's going to be so *interesting.*"

I laugh. "You know, I'm not avoiding it because I think the bees are boring. More like . . . *terrifying.*"

"You might appreciate them more if you see them up close," Hazel says.

I grimace. "I'll watch from the window."

"Your loss." She heads to the back of the house and returns in a few minutes wearing her bee suit—a white one-piece coverall. She wears gloves and a brimmed hat with a mesh surround.

"You look like an astronaut bride," I say.

Hazel grins. "I think you mean an *amazing* astronaut bride."

She steps outside and picks up a stainless steel container she calls a smoker. Hazel loads it with wood chips and lights them on fire. Then she starts to puff air through the smoker. I shake my head. This is the big difference between Astrid and my parents. I can't imagine them letting me set something on fire, much less a fire that would prevent me from being stung by my own personal fifty thousand bees. Hazel acts like she's done it a hundred times, which maybe she has.

I read in one of Hazel's books that smoke makes bees less likely to attack. Bees think there is a fire and start gorging themselves on honey. They're too busy to be interested in stinging. Also, the smoke masks the bees' pheromones so they can't send out their "danger" scent and warn the other bees. Either way, Hazel says it works, and I'm not going to argue.

Hazel approaches the beehive from behind and adds a few puffs of smoke at the entrance. She waits for a few seconds and then removes the outer cover, which she sets on the grass next to her. Then she uses the smoker again before removing the inner cover.

When Hazel opens the top of the beehive, I brace myself against a wave of dizziness. I'm not sure what to expect. Maybe the bees will fly out of the hive, surrounding Hazel like a cloud. But that doesn't happen. Some fly out, but no more than usual. From here, they seem mildly curious but not angry.

Hazel takes the boxes apart, sometimes using the smoker and waiting before doing the next section. When she gets to the bottom box, she pulls out the frames and looks at them carefully. She replaces them before moving to the next box. Her movements are smooth and confident.

The front door swings open, and Astrid comes in. She's carrying a gym bag and yoga mat.

"Hi, Meg," Astrid says.

"Hi," I answer. "Hazel is outside checking the bees."

Astrid joins me at the window, watching. Hazel sees her mom and waves.

"She's so happy out there with her bees," says Astrid.

I nod. "She really knows what she's doing."

Astrid smiles. "In Newford, there are a lot of urban beekeepers. Our friend Claudia is a master beekeeper. She said she'd teach Hazel everything she knew."

"It worked," I say. "'Cause Hazel knows a ton about them."

"Hazel used to give talks on them at school every year. I think she hoped they would help her make friends. It didn't work out like that, of course." Astrid sighs. "She's always related much better to adults."

Astrid is talking in a way that makes Hazel sound completely awkward. I feel the need to stick up for her.

"She told me about all those clubs she was in," I say. "Chess and stargazing? I bet she had lots of friends in those."

Astrid's eyes look watery. "Sure, she was in those clubs—but she was the only member. I hoped that with a fresh start, things would be different. Better."

Hazel always talks about Newford like it's a perfect place. But when I think back, she never mentioned any friends at all, except Claudia. She talked about bees, but she never mentioned another kid.

Astrid pats my arm. "I didn't mean to make you worry.

After all, she has you! I'm so glad you two are working on this project together."

Astrid offers me tea, and I say okay. I'm still thinking about what she said. Hazel didn't have any friends at all in Newford, except for Claudia. So why did she talk about all those clubs? Why did she lie about her dad?

I watch Hazel as she continues the inspection. When she finishes, she comes inside.

"Did you get stung?" I ask.

"No stings," says Hazel happily. "And they look healthy. Soon it will get warm, and the queen will start laying tons of eggs. It's going to be great."

Astrid pours lemonade and gives us each a bowl of organic puffed wheat squares. She beams at us, sitting at the table, with an extra-sunshiny smile for Hazel. It's a loving kind of look, a mom kind of look.

Hazel eyes her suspiciously. "Why are you looking at me like that?"

"No reason," Astrid says. But when Hazel looks back at her paper, Astrid gives me a wink.

I know what the wink means. I can tell Astrid wants everything to be okay. She thinks I'm Hazel's friend.

And the weird thing is, I think she may be right.

CHAPTER

19

*B*zzz.

I don't see who starts it.

Our essays on the Industrial Revolution are due next week. Mr. Thornton is out in the hall, calling us one by one to give individual feedback on our rough drafts. Those of us left in the classroom are supposed to be writing.

Bzzz. From somewhere to my right.

And then another one, from somewhere behind me.

People are giggling, turning their heads to try to see who is doing it. Everyone but Hazel, who is looking straight down at her paper.

It quiets for a moment, and people turn back to their papers. But then it starts again.

Bzzz.

                Bzzz.

                                Bzzzzz!

I can't tell who it is. It might be just a few, scattered around the room. It might be everyone. It's happening more frequently now. Maybe that's part of the plan, or maybe more people are joining in, like it's some kind of game. I hear one that I swear comes from Beatrix, but when I look at her, she's innocently sipping from her Uncle Bean's cup. I'm pretty sure I hear one from Zoe.

It's almost quiet enough to miss. *Almost.* But I know I'm not imagining it. And Hazel knows it's for her. She hasn't turned her head once, but the back of her neck matches her magenta sweater.

bzzz.   *bZZZ!*

                    Bzzz.

                              Bzzzzz.

BZZZZ.

                    Bzzzzz.

Almost the entire class is doing it now. There are barely any quiet spaces between the buzzing sounds. Some kids aren't even trying to be subtle. Ryan holds his hand over his mouth: *Cough-cough-bzzz.*

The door opens, and Mr. Thornton sticks his head in the room. "Meg, your turn."

When we get into the hall, I make sure the door is shut tight behind me.

"Mr. Thornton," I say. "Something is happening in class."

He tilts his head to the side, then glances through the door's glass panel. From the outside, he can't hear the buzzing.

"What do you mean?" he asks.

I haven't thought this through. I don't know how to report it when it's not one person doing it—it's almost everyone. But the heart of the problem is between Beatrix and Hazel. Maybe there's a way to tell him without getting Beatrix in trouble.

He's looking at me expectantly.

"There's a problem," I say. "Between two girls—"

Mr. Thornton holds up his hand to stop me. "Is someone in danger of being physically harmed?"

I'm puzzled for a minute, before I understand what he's asking. "No, but—"

He holds up his hand again. "Is someone being bothered because of their race or orientation?"

I shake my head. "Nothing like that."

He sighs. "Then please encourage them to come to me directly. I don't like to get involved in thirdhand drama."

I bite the skin on the side of my thumb. But, for once, it's not from being nervous. It's because I am mad. I like Mr. Thornton, but I hate that he called it *drama*. Just because it's two girls having a problem does not mean it's drama. No one ever uses that word to describe boys disagreeing, unless it's sort of a sneaky way to tell them that they are acting "like a girl."

I can barely listen as he talks about my transition words and how I could combine two sentences with a semicolon. I don't know anyone who uses semicolons.

I return to the classroom, and sure enough, the buzzing is still going strong. It continues for the rest of literacy block. I can't imagine how upset Hazel must be. I feel dizzy, and I know the buzzing isn't for me.

When the bell rings, I let out a breath I hadn't realized I was holding. But as soon as I step into the hallway, I hear it again. It rises reedily above conversations, slamming locker doors, and sneakers squeaking in the hall. I don't see Hazel until lunch, but the buzzing travels around the edges of my day.

In the cafeteria, it starts up again. This time I see who does it first. It's Beatrix. I *knew* it.

"Come on," I say. "That's not nice."

"Relax, Meg," says Beatrix. "It's just a joke."

I can see Hazel across the lunchroom. She's absorbed in her book. I want to believe she doesn't hear it. But her bright-red face and neck give it away. I think about what Astrid said about Hazel not having friends back in Newford, and anger bubbles inside me. Beatrix shouldn't pick on Hazel. She hasn't done anything wrong. The only thing she's done is try to make friends and be a nice person. She doesn't deserve to be treated this way.

"Jokes are supposed to be funny," I say. "This isn't."

"She probably likes it," Beatrix says innocently. "She wants people to like bees."

Arshi and Zoe come from the lunch line then, and I can almost block it out. But as lunch goes on, the buzzing gets stronger—louder than this morning. Almost everyone in the seventh grade is making random buzzing noises, but the cafeteria monitors don't seem to notice.

The sound surrounds us. It makes me feel like I'm trapped in a real beehive. Even though seats aren't technically assigned, we sit at the same tables every day. Tyler and the soccer boys who all have the same haircut, Ryan and his friends who wear shirts with funny sayings every day, Cora and the kids who do academic competitions. We carry out our jobs just like the bees in a colony. The thought suddenly hits me: the seventh grade is like a superorganism. And Beatrix is our queen.

I glance at Hazel again. She looks so calm, reading. But when I see the title of her book, I can't believe it. It's one with honey bees on the cover. Not one bee or two. The book jacket is covered in bees. I've seen it at her house before, and I remember the funny title, *Honeybee Democracy*. And here she is, reading it right smack in the middle of the cafeteria.

I don't get it. Why would she call attention to herself

by reading a bee book? It's like she doesn't care what other people think.

That's not it. She *does* care. I can tell by her bright-red face. I can tell by her hunched shoulders. But Hazel cares more about doing what she wants to do. She loves bees, and no one's going to stop her from reading about them. She's sending the whole cafeteria a message. It makes me want to do a personal cheer for her, right then and there.

Beatrix follows my eyes. "Bee Girl is reading a bee book. How special."

I know the answer, but I need to hear her say it. "Was the buzzing your idea?"

Beatrix smirks. "What if it was?"

My head hurts. "But why? How?"

Beatrix shrugs. "I told a few people, and they told a few others. I can't help that word got around."

I frown.

Beatrix sighs. "You two are science class buddies. I thought you might be on the side of the bees."

The anger in my chest feels like boiling. What Beatrix is doing is wrong.

I don't want to choose sides. But maybe I'm going to have to.

CHAPTER

20

ANTHROPOMORPHISM

Ms. Dupart underlines the word on the board. The entire class looks confused. Anthropo-what?

Ms. Dupart caps her marker with a *click*. "Can anyone define it?"

Alfredo raises his hand. "Is it the study of humans?"

Ms. Dupart points her marker at him. "That's anthropology. But you're right about 'anthro,' which is a good clue." She writes *human* on the board underneath *anthro*.

She looks around, but no one has another guess.

"'Morph' means 'shape,' and 'ism' means 'belief in,'"

she continues. "So the word technically means 'belief in human shape.' A better definition is this."

ANTHROPOMORPHISM
ATTRIBUTING HUMAN CHARACTERISTICS TO SOMETHING

She taps the board. "In our case, the 'something' is the animals we are studying. What do you think? Is anthropomorphism good or bad?"

A boy named Finn Graham raises his hand. He doesn't talk much, but I've noticed he wears a different St. Louis Cardinals shirt each day. "I think it's good, because people care more when they have something in common."

"So anthropomorphism can help with feeling connected to animals," Ms. Dupart says.

"Well, I think it's bad," says Ava Watts. "We can't be objective if we're always thinking about how animals are like us."

Ms. Dupart nods. "Anyone else?"

Hazel raises her hand. "I think it's okay for pets, like if you dress up your dog in a cute outfit. But in science, it could be bad if you aren't paying attention to the special things that an animal can do."

"Can you think of an example?"

Hazel frowns for a minute, then brightens. "Bee eyes work differently from human eyes. Bees can't see red, but they can see UV light, which helps them fly right to where the nectar is on a flower. So if I'm looking at flowers in my yard, I could say 'bees like the orange ones,' when it's more complicated than that."

The mention of bees makes me brace myself. The last thing I want to hear is another round of buzzing. But there aren't enough seventh graders to get it going. Mr. Thornton's class is one thing, but even Ryan wouldn't dare buzz right in front of Ms. Dupart's nose.

Ms. Dupart beams. "That's a great example. So this word is something I'd like everyone to keep in mind as they are working. We can find ways that anthropomorphism is good and bad. But the important thing is that it's a very common thing—a very *human* thing to do. It's something to be aware of. Let's have a few more examples."

The conversation goes on, but I look out the window, half listening. Even though it's only February, the weather has warmed enough to bloom the flowers of the redbud tree. I might not have noticed except for Hazel being so excited for spring and all the flowers her bees are going to discover in Willow Pond.

Hazel loves bees so much, she would probably turn into one if she could. The idea makes me shudder.

Usually, learning the facts makes me feel better. I wish I could say that's been true about the bees. The more I know, the more nervous I feel. It's not really about the stinging anymore. Hazel is right that stinging is pretty rare, all things considered. It's the beehive itself that contains thousands of bees in a dark, enclosed space. I don't know how Hazel can handle the thought of it. I may be anthropomorphizing, but the idea of living in a hive with fifty thousand crawling, buzzing siblings makes me want to run screaming from the room.

"All right," Ms. Dupart says. "Time to work on your research."

I pull out the notes I was working on yesterday. I'm fascinated by the queen. I thought maybe queens were born from special eggs, but they aren't. All female eggs start out the same, but queens are fed royal jelly exclusively when they are developing. Other than that, queens are random. They aren't chosen because they're special. They're made through luck.

I've heard the expression "queen bee" before. It means a girl who likes to be in charge and run things, and maybe is a bit mean sometimes. It's a phrase that gives me a bad feeling. We don't have a word for boys who do that. I've heard "alpha male," but I don't think it's the same thing. Maybe the animal kingdom has no boy version of a queen bee. Or maybe, when a boy acts that way, it's considered normal, and we don't even notice. It makes me wonder what Mr. Thornton would have said if I told him the problem was between two boys. I don't think he would have called it *drama*.

Ms. Dupart wants us to be careful about anthropomorphizing, but I can't help thinking again of Beatrix as the queen bee of Willow Pond Middle. I wish I could figure out what makes Beatrix the way she is. Is it luck, or is it something more? I don't know if she could change. I don't know if she would want to.

That afternoon feels like spring, and even Bart and Lola can tell. Bart is so excited, he keeps getting tangled in his leash.

Beatrix laughs and helps unwrap it from his leg.

"You goof," she says lovingly, scratching him behind his ears. She's so patient and kind with dogs. If only she could be like that all the time.

"How's dance elective?" I ask. Beatrix hasn't talked about it much lately.

She spins while she answers. Lola runs in a perfect circle around her, barking. "Good! Coach Alinaghi is letting me do my individual piece. You should come to the recital, even though you aren't in the class anymore."

"Okay," I say. "And you have a spring recital for ballet, too?"

Beatrix stops twirling. "Rehearsals constantly, six days a week. My feet are disgusting."

Ballet does strange things to a person's feet. I'm not sure if Beatrix is grossed out by it or semi-bragging about how hard she works. Maybe both.

I stop to fix Bart's leash, which is twisted around his leg again.

We run to finish the loop around the field. The air feels different in spring, softer somehow. We head home slowly, letting Bart and Lola take their time sniffing the grass.

"How's your class with Bee Girl?" Beatrix asks.

I sigh. "You mean Hazel?"

"Yeah, Hazel," says Beatrix. "Is there another Bee Girl I don't know about?"

This whole thing is getting old. "No, there's no other Bee Girl."

"Good." Beatrix nods. "We don't need another one. Besides, maybe soon she won't be Bee Girl anymore."

I frown. "What is that supposed to mean?"

"Never mind," says Beatrix. "The point is, the neighbors are not happy about the bees. It's just a matter of time until someone complains to Mrs. Johnston again, and then the bees will be out of here. That's why everyone is buzzing in the cafeteria. They want those bees to go away."

I don't understand why Beatrix is so mad.

"The bees haven't hurt anyone," I say.

She glares at me. "Not *yet*, you mean."

I feel my heart beat faster. "If they use their stingers, they die. A worker bee's stinger is connected to her guts and other inside parts, and that gets left behind when she stings."

Beatrix is looking at me like I'm completely weird. "That is so gross, Meg."

"I learned about it," I say. "In my research. It's interesting, Beatrix. The venom keeps pumping as long as the stinger is embedded. So if you ever do get stung, you should pull it out right away."

She sighs loudly. "What are you even talking about?"

I bring my thumb toward my mouth but then pull it away. "I'm just saying that the bees are interesting, that's all."

Beatrix shudders. "I have no idea what you're saying. All I know is this: bees have stingers so they can sting. It's a fact."

I shake my head. "No, Beatrix. That's what I'm trying to tell you. Stinging is their last resort. It's actually science. You can't argue with that."

"My yard backs up to theirs," says Beatrix. "Do you want my family getting stung?"

"Of course I don't!"

Beatrix shrugs. "Can you guarantee they won't be?"

I sigh. Of course I can't say they won't get stung, but it's not right to act like that's all bees ever do.

"No. I can't guarantee it."

"Okay, then," says Beatrix, like it proves her point.

"But—"

Beatrix shakes her head. "But *nothing*, Meg. I know you don't want to choose sides, but it's going to come down to it at some point."

"That's not fair," I say. "It isn't about sides."

"I'm not going to change my mind about this," she says. It sounds like a warning. She loops Lola's leash around her hand and then unloops it.

"Come on," I say finally. "Let's run."

We don't talk the rest of the way home.

CHAPTER

21

Days pass, and the buzzing doesn't stop. If anything, it gets worse. A few teachers have started to notice. They think it's just a trend, not something directed at Hazel. So they say, "Let's settle down, guys." This makes it stop for a while, but once we step into the halls or move on to the next class, it starts again.

Hazel and I don't talk about it. I'm afraid to embarrass her by bringing it up. She never mentions it to me. But each time I hear a buzz, I see her face get red. I don't think it can get any worse.

But then the whispering starts. Not *to* Hazel but *about* her.

I hear it all day but can't quite make out what people

are saying. Every time I get close, the conversation stops suddenly. I even hear Hazel's name when I pass by a knot of sixth graders. *Sixth graders!* Usually, no one tells them anything, so this means whatever it is, it's big. My stomach twists all morning.

At lunch, Arshi spills the news.

"Hazel made up all that stuff about her dad and that octopus," Arshi says. "Everyone is talking about it."

I freeze. I knew about that already, but I thought I was the only one.

Zoe frowns, adjusting her side braid. "Wait. Which part is made up? The dad part or the octopus part?"

Arshi shrugs. "Both, I think. Apparently, she is a total liar."

"But why?" Zoe asks.

"Probably because she wanted to make up a reason why he's gone," says Beatrix. "I mean, it sounds a lot better than saying he lives in Ohio."

Then I remember. I'm *not* the only person. I told Beatrix that day when we were walking the dogs. I wanted Beatrix to understand that I didn't think Hazel was perfect or that anyone was. I never thought she would use that against Hazel.

"It's sad, when you think about it," says Zoe.

Beatrix's eyes glint. "It's *scary*, when you think about it. She's the one saying that the bees are safe. How can we believe anything she says?"

I watch Hazel. She's sitting alone at the table and looks

miserable. I don't know what happened to the girls she usually sits with. Maybe they decided to ditch her.

Then Cora shows up, holding her striped lunch bag. She sits with Hazel, and at first I'm relieved. Then I see Cora's expression. Behind her purple glasses, her eyes are worried.

Cora leans across the table. I'm too far to hear what she says, but she's wiggling her fingers like they're tentacles and I think I see her mouth the word *octopus*.

Hazel draws back like she's been slapped. She seems to shrink inside herself, like her dragon sweater is suddenly three sizes too big.

When Cora stops talking, Hazel nods miserably. Then she stands up and walks out of the cafeteria, leaving her tray behind.

I look at my lunch. There's no flavor left.

It's my fault. The dizziness comes, and I try to breathe through it. I can't faint, not in the cafeteria.

The bell rings, and Arshi and Zoe dump their trays. When Beatrix stands up, I ask her to wait. I have to know.

"You were the one who started the rumor, weren't you?" I ask.

Beatrix's eyes widen. Then she shakes her head slowly.

"No, Meg," she says patiently. "*You're* the one who started it."

My face prickles hot. I bite my thumb.

"I didn't start a rumor," I say. "You know that. I told

you because you were upset. You were crying because you thought Hazel was perfect."

"That's not how I remember it," she says.

I gulp.

"Don't worry," she says. "I'm sure it won't get out that you were the one who started it."

She walks away. For once, I don't follow.

CHAPTER

22

That afternoon, Hazel isn't in science elective.

After school, I look for Mrs. Bailey's car, but then I remember. This weekend the Baileys are going to their beach house. Beatrix got checked out after fifth period. I'm supposed to walk home today.

The air is sweet, and the sky is blue, but my bad mood won't shake off. I know it's my fault. I should never have told Beatrix about Hazel lying. I did it so Beatrix would feel better. I never meant for it to become a rumor. But now it's all the school is talking about, and that is one hundred percent entirely my fault.

When I get home, Dad and Conrad are in the kitchen.

Dad stirs a pot of tomato sauce, and Conrad leans against the counter, drinking a soda.

"It's a special night," Dad says.

I run through my mental calendar. It's not a birthday or a holiday. My parents' anniversary isn't until June. I look at Conrad for help, but he shrugs.

"I realized something momentous." Dad gestures with his spoon for emphasis, which sends tomato sauce splatter flying. "Oops." He wipes the mess before continuing. "Ask me where Elsie is."

"Day care?" I ask.

"No," Dad says. "She is having a sleepover with Grandma Lou."

"Fun," I say. I used to love doing that when I was little.

"What's more," Dad continues, "my teenager and my almost-teenager don't have any plans. The stars have aligned, and with very little planning or forethought, all four of us will be home tonight. We will be taking full advantage of the opportunity," Dad says solemnly.

I have a sinking feeling. I'm pretty sure his grand plans will involve organizing the attic or power washing the deck.

I look at him suspiciously. "What do you mean?"

"For dinner, I'm making pizza," he says.

"Okay." This part is good news. I love Dad's home-made pizzas. Clearly, he is leading up to something else.

He smiles sheepishly. "Play-testing. You, Conrad, Mom, and me. Please? I'll treat you to ice cream later."

Games with my parents and Conrad with ice cream after? That's a good deal.

"I'm in," I say.

"Whew," Dad says. "I'm tired of playing with stuffed animals."

Conrad and I help get the pizzas in the oven. Mom comes home and seems happy and relaxed. We take the pizzas upstairs to Dad's office. He hands out the Evildoer cards and explains the rules.

"I don't know," says Mom, arranging her cards. "I don't like these games where the idea is to do bad things to the people you're playing with."

Conrad scrunches his forehead. "Every board game that exists is about doing bad things to the people you're playing with."

I laugh. "He has a point."

"Not *every* game," Mom protests. "What about Monopoly?"

Dad groans. This is a long-standing argument between them. He says Monopoly is the worst, most boring game ever created, and that it needs more opportunity for players to have interaction and conflict. But for some reason, Mom loves it.

"There are so many better, more modern games," Dad complains. "Why is my beloved wife so fixated on Monopoly?"

"Monopoly is peaceful, with cute street names and

rows of tiny houses," says Mom. "It's not about messing with the other players. Tennessee Avenue. Marvin Gardens."

"You must not remember what it's like to play with Conrad," I say. "When he buys Broadway and Park Place, it's absolutely so he can mess with the rest of us."

Conrad looks smug. "It's not my fault I invest wisely."

"Conflict exists in board games to make them interesting," says Dad. "What would be the point of playing if there weren't a few bumps in the road?"

"There must be a game without conflict," says Mom. "What about solitaire?"

"Nope," I say. "You play against the deck, so it's like your enemy is yourself."

"I know," says Mom. "Candy Land!"

There is a silence while everyone tries to think of a way to argue with her, but no one comes up with anything.

"But Candy Land is for kids Elsie's age," Conrad says.

"I'm still right," says Mom. "An extra scoop of ice cream for me, please."

"You win," says Dad. He leans over and kisses Mom on the side of her head.

Conrad and I look at each other. Secretly, it's okay that Mom and Dad love each other so much. But we can't let them know that.

"Gross, you guys," I say.

"Yeah," says Conrad. "Ew."

I study my cards. Dad's made a lot of progress from the last time we played. For Dad's games, the rules always state that the youngest player goes first, which I have always loved, because it feels like it is written especially for me. I guess when Elsie gets old enough to play, she will feel like it was written for her. But for now, I use it to my advantage. I play a card that makes Conrad give me half his treasure.

"Ugh," he says. "That's a terrible start."

"Not for me," I say, and move my piece on the board.

The game flows pretty well, and there are only a few places where Dad stops us so he can make notes.

Playing in Dad's office is cozy. It feels like the old days, when it was just the four of us. Back then, Dad, Mom, and Conrad were my entire world. When I was really little, each day seemed to last so long, because almost everything I did was new and exciting. Mom and Dad were like giants, because they were always in the very center of my universe. That's how Elsie feels now, probably. It's the four of us, plus her tigers and Grandma Lou.

But as the world got wider—with school, friends, and activities—Mom and Dad seemed to shrink a bit. They didn't change, but the world I live in is so much bigger. Sometimes it's uncomfortable to see how little space Mom and Dad take up in the big, wide world.

The game finishes, and somehow Conrad comes from

behind and wins. He brags so much, it's like he won the world championship.

"All right, everyone," says Dad. "Give me a couple of minutes to make notes, and then we'll go out for broccoli."

"Ice cream!" I say.

"Oh, all right—ice cream."

I go to my room to grab a fleece.

"Meg! It's your friend!" Conrad yells from downstairs.

I frown. Beatrix should be at the beach already, but maybe they had to cancel. Maybe she's here to apologize about what happened today at lunch.

I clomp down the stairs. At the bottom, I skid to a stop. Standing in our living room is Hazel. Mom's standing with her, looking concerned.

My eyes widen. Hazel's never been to my house before. We always meet at her place, because that's where the bees are.

"Hey," I say.

When I look at Hazel's face, I get nervous. Her eyes are rimmed in red, and it looks like she's been crying. Guilt flashes deep within me. I wonder if she's found out who started the rumor.

"What's wrong?" I ask.

She opens her mouth, but no words come out. She holds up a paper, folded into thirds. Instead of answering, she bursts into tears.

I walk over to her. If she were Beatrix, I would hug

her. But Hazel and I have never hugged before. I put my hand out and kind of pat her on the arm. "It's okay, Hazel. Whatever it is, it will be okay."

She's still sobbing but manages to choke out a few words. "It's a letter from the town. It says I can't keep my bees."

I look at Mom for help, but she is already wrapping Hazel in a hug.

CHAPTER

23

Dad, who seems bewildered about the crying girl in his house, does not ask questions when Mom tells him Hazel will be joining us for ice cream. Astrid is working late, so Mom makes Hazel call and leave her a message before we can go.

We load into the van. A few times, Mom tries to start a conversation. But somehow, every topic she lands on— science elective, Hazel's new house, what Hazel and her mom like to do on weekends—leads back to the bees and a fresh wave of tears from Hazel. Luckily, the drive to Cooper's isn't far.

After we settle with our cones into the large booth

near the window, Dad swallows a very large bite of his pineapple-raisin and turns to Hazel.

"What's this about the bees?" he asks.

Mom looks worried, as if the question might launch Hazel into tears once more, but it doesn't. Hazel pulls the letter from her coat pocket and hands it over to Dad. He reads it, with Conrad looking over his shoulder. Then he passes the letter to Mom.

"This stinks," Conrad says. "So you'll have to get rid of them, huh?"

Hazel sighs. "I don't know."

"Can I see the letter?" I ask.

She hands it to me. It's wrinkled, but I do my best to spread it out on the table.

```
To Astrid James
7311 Maple Way
Willow Pond, NC


Re: unauthorized beekeeping


Please refer to your neighborhood rules
and regulations--specifically, the
following are prohibited:


Section (5.21): activities which are a
nuisance to others;
```

Section (8.9): plants, animals, or other
activities that are determined to be
harmful, dangerous, unsightly;

Section (12.12): activities that decrease
the enjoyment of the Willow Pond
community.

If corrective action is not taken within
10 days, you will be fined.

I read the letter, and then I read it again. I don't understand all the words, but I know a letter like this can't be good.

I frown at an unfamiliar word. "What does nu-ih-sance mean?"

"Nuisance," Mom corrects me. It sounds like *new-since*. "It means something that bothers others."

Dad points his spoon at Hazel. "If I got that letter, the first thing I would do is call Town Hall. Find out who sent it and on what authority. Then I would find out if there's some kind of way to meet with whoever made the complaint."

"Hazel didn't say anything about fighting this," says Mom. "Don't jump ahead."

"Of course they're going to fight it," I say. "The bees are important to Hazel."

Hazel's whole face looks crumpled. She takes another bite of her cone.

"Now, honey," says Mom. "It's an official letter, addressed to her mom. So they'll need to talk it over before making a decision."

I want to read it again. I look it over five times before I say anything.

"I think this was written by someone who doesn't understand bees very well," I say. "Especially if they think the bees are bothering others. Have they done anything that bothers your neighbors?"

"I don't know," says Hazel glumly.

"Maybe we can find out," I say. I point to the next section. "Second, it says harmful, dangerous, or unsightly animals are not allowed."

"Harmful," Conrad says. "It would be hard to argue against that one. Bees have stingers, and that's for harming things."

I shake my head. "I don't know. They don't sting very often. It doesn't seem like that would be enough to call them harmful."

Dad chews thoughtfully. "Go on. What else?"

"Dangerous," Hazel says.

"Isn't that the same thing as 'harmful'?" Conrad asks.

"Maybe," I say. "But I think we could argue that, too. Bees sting defensively, so they aren't dangerous unless they're trying to protect themselves. And the last one, unsightly? The beehives aren't ugly. They blend in. The first time I went to Hazel's, I kept looking around for the beehive, because I didn't notice it."

Hazel smiles for the first time all night. "Really?"

I smile back. "Really. You didn't tell me what it would look like."

"I thought you would know it was the thing with the bees flying around it," Hazel jokes.

I grin. I don't mind her teasing me—I'm just happy to see her smile.

"Finally, it says that beehives decrease enjoyment," I say. "I don't know if that's true."

"Bees *increase* enjoyment—for Hazel anyway," says Conrad.

I bite the skin on the side of my thumb, thinking hard. It's true that bees increase enjoyment for Hazel, but the rest of the neighborhood should be happy, too.

"Listen," Mom says, putting down her ice cream. "Let's not rush into anything. I'm sure the town has reasons for their rules. It isn't worth making waves and upsetting people over something like this."

I frown at Mom. The bees are everything to Hazel. Doesn't Mom see that?

"Bees help flowers grow," says Hazel, sounding more confident. "And people with gardens sometimes get bigger vegetables when bees are kept nearby."

"See? That's not harmful," says Conrad.

"It's the opposite of harmful," I say. "We'll talk to the town and make them change their minds."

Hazel uses a wadded-up napkin to wipe her eyes.

"Do you think we can do it?" she asks.

"Definitely," I say.

But when I see Mom's face, it's full of worry—and then I'm not so sure.

After ice cream, we drop off Hazel at her house and make sure she gets inside safely. When we get home, Mom sits with me on the couch.

"Look," she says. "I'm worried about you getting involved in this trouble with the town. If Hazel's bees break the rules, she shouldn't be allowed to have them."

"But the town is wrong about the bees," I say. "That's what I was trying to say at Cooper's. If you look at the rules they listed, they don't apply."

Mom's face looks pinched. "Someone posted about it on the neighborhood group. There are already twenty comments."

I know all about the neighborhood group. Sometimes Dad reads us the posts at breakfast. Usually it's complaints about bringing in trash cans from the curb in a timely fashion. Sometimes it's "gentle reminders" about cleaning up after pets. One time a post complaining about Christmas lights left hanging until March got fifty-seven replies.

It seems like it would be easier if people talked to each other directly.

"What do the posts say?" I ask. "Are people worried about being stung?"

"That's a big part of it," says Mom. "I know you think they don't sting very often, but some people think that even once is too much. Other people are talking about property values or whether bees making honey counts as a business activity."

I frown. "They haven't even harvested the honey yet. They haven't tried to sell it."

Mom sighs. "I know you're upset, sweetie, but it's important to listen to what others have to say here. There are a lot of strong feelings on the website, and I don't want you caught in the middle of things. People get upset when property values start getting involved."

"I don't even know what 'property values' means," I say.

"It means how much the house and its land are worth," Mom says. "It's one of those things that can be open to interpretation. For example, some people like to be near a school so it's convenient for their children. Other people don't like the added noise and traffic a school can bring."

Suddenly, I'm suspicious. That sounds like real estate stuff.

"Who posted about it first? Was it Mrs. Bailey?"

Mom shifts, looking uncomfortable. "Lots of people posted, Meg."

"But Mrs. Bailey started it, right?" I ask.

Mom's face tells the answer.

"It's not fair!" I say. "Not to Hazel, not to the bees."

Mom brushes my hair from my forehead. "I know it doesn't seem fair to you, but you have to try to see the other side. Think about how Beatrix would feel if you argued against her mom, against their family."

"Maybe people will get out all their feelings online and then decide not to bother the bees." Even as I say it, I'm not so sure.

Mom taps the side of her mug, looking doubtful. "Maybe."

I wish it would all go away. But instead, I have a bad feeling that the bee problem is going to go from bad to worse.

CHAPTER

24

It's Monday morning and I'm moving slowly. I'm putting my cereal bowl in the dishwasher when Mom's phone chimes.

Mom looks at it, frowning. "The Baileys have an emergency, so they can't give you a ride this morning."

I wonder if they decided to stay one more night at their beach house. "Did she say anything else?"

Mom shakes her head. "Hope everything is all right."

I squeeze my thumb. I've been half waiting for The Freeze to start. Maybe today is the day.

Mom glances at the clock. "I'll drop you on my way to work. Ready to go?"

I grab my backpack and head to the garage. In the car, Mom hasn't even backed out of the driveway before she turns the conversation to what happened Friday night.

"Of course it's okay to be friends with Hazel," Mom says. "And I know she has strong feelings about this. But you have to remember that no one loves Willow Pond more than the Baileys. They have the town's best interests at heart."

I pull at a string on my backpack that's coming loose. It's true that I don't understand this property-value stuff. But something about the whole thing seems wrong. Beatrix didn't even want to listen to anything scientific about the bees. Her mind is already made up—about the bees and about Hazel. It doesn't seem fair.

The drop-off line moves quickly, and before I know it, I'm getting out. I give Mom a quick wave goodbye.

"Think about what I said," Mom says before she pulls away.

Beatrix isn't at school when the bell rings for literacy block. I chew the skin on the inside of my thumb, listening to Mr. Thornton introducing our unit on North Carolina history. It's hard to be excited or pay attention, but I try. By the end of the discussion, he is talking about Orville and Wilbur Wright. This would be interesting if I hadn't heard it a million times already. Every kid in North Carolina learns about their historic flight near Kitty Hawk, and every fifth grader at Willow Pond Elementary visits the Outer Banks on a field trip. It's all the same stuff we've been learning for ages.

But Mr. Thornton is excited, gesturing wildly, as he describes the different aviators at the time who were racing to be the first in flight.

Ryan raises his hand. He didn't spike up his hair today, so it looks soft and floppy. "Mr. Thornton?"

Mr. Thornton beams, delighted that someone seems interested. "Yes, Mr. Hong?"

Ryan grins. "I know why Orville and Wilbur were the first aviators."

Mr. Thornton looks at Ryan blankly.

"Because if someone else flew first, it wouldn't be Wright. Get it? *Wright.*"

A few kids giggle, and others groan. But before Mr. Thornton can respond, the classroom door opens, and Beatrix sweeps in. She hands him a pass from the office and makes her way to her desk.

"What happened?" I whisper.

Beatrix plops her backpack on the floor and sits down. She leans slightly toward me but speaks loud enough that the kids around us can hear. "We were in the hospital all night!"

Everyone turns toward Beatrix in surprise.

Mr. Thornton, at the front of the classroom, says, "People? Let's get back on track."

"I'll tell you later," Beatrix loud-whispers.

The rest of the class, my mind races. Was it one of her brothers in the hospital? Her grandpa? By the time the bell rings I'm impatient. I can't wait to hear everything. But instead of telling me, she picks up her backpack and walks to the hall.

I follow behind her. "Beatrix, what's going on? Who was in the hospital? What happened?"

Finally, Beatrix answers. "It was Rocco."

"Oh, Rocco!" I say, grinning. I'm so relieved that it isn't something more serious. He probably got into something in the pantry and stuffed himself silly.

Beatrix looks at me sharply. "Why are you sounding so happy about it? Rocco is a part of our family, Meg."

"I'm not happy it was Rocco," I say. "Of course not. Is he okay?"

Beatrix sniffs. "Well, it was a very big deal. We got back from the beach in the afternoon, and everyone was running around unpacking and everything. The dogs were in the backyard because they were all sandy, and Mom wanted to wash them before they came inside. But when I checked on Rocco, he was standing there panting, like he couldn't breathe."

"Oh no," I say.

Beatrix bites her lip, remembering. "He was acting really out of it. And when we got in the car, he kept closing his eyes. Only my mom said not to let him fall asleep because maybe he was going into shock. So I kept holding him and saying, 'Rocco, Rocco, stay awake.' His face was puffy, and his eyes were little slits."

I think of sweet, silly Rocco, who loves salami and

belly rubs. The idea of him struggling to breathe makes me feel like crying.

"So what happened after that?" I ask.

"The vet said he'll be okay," says Beatrix. "He just needs to take it easy."

"That's good," I say. "Do they know what caused it?"

"Oh, I thought I said." Beatrix pauses dramatically. "He was stung by bees."

I'm shocked. "All that from a bee sting?"

"From a *bunch* of bee stings," she corrects me. "His whole face swelled up like a balloon."

"Poor Rocco," I say.

"I told you those bees are dangerous," Beatrix says. "Hazel is putting our whole neighborhood in danger."

"Wait a minute," I say. "It was *Hazel's* bees?"

Beatrix scowls. "Really, Meg? What other bees do you know about?"

I want to tell her they could be anyone's bees. But it's not the right time.

We walk to class together and say goodbye at the doorway. I feel terrible for Rocco. I feel terrible for Hazel, too. Whether her bees hurt Rocco or not, that's what the Baileys think. That means the whole town will think that, too. There's no way Hazel will be able to keep her bees after that.

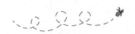

At lunch, Beatrix repeats the story for Zoe and Arshi, who are stunned.

"I never knew that a dog could be allergic to bees," says Arshi.

Zoe shakes her head. "Anyone can be allergic. I can't believe she's allowed to keep them."

But I've been thinking. I finish chewing my apple and clear my throat.

"I was wondering about something," I say. "How do you know they belonged to Hazel?"

Beatrix flips her ponytail. "Of course they did. Whose else would they be?"

I want to explain that bees can fly miles from their hive. So there's no way to know if the bees were Hazel's or somebody else's. But I'm stopped by Beatrix's frown. It's not directed at me. She's looking over my shoulder, so I turn to see. It's Hazel, walking by our table with her lunch tray.

"Liar," Beatrix says as Hazel passes.

Hazel wheels around. "What did you say?"

"I said *liar*," Beatrix repeats. "You're a liar, Bee Girl."

Hazel stomps over to our table. The sounds of the cafeteria drop away as the other kids sense something happening.

"Stop it," Hazel says. "I'm tired of it. Stop buzzing at me. Stop telling people I'm a liar."

"But you *are* a liar," Beatrix says. "Everyone knows it."

"I don't know what you mean," says Hazel. "I don't know what I ever did to you. I just want you to stop."

"Then stop lying, liar," Beatrix says.

"I—" Hazel starts.

Beatrix interrupts. "Let's see: You said the bees won't hurt anyone, but they almost killed my dog. You said your dad lives on a submarine when he really lives in Ohio."

Hazel freezes. She opens her mouth, but no words come.

"I don't blame him," Beatrix says. "If I had a weird kid like you, I'd move to Ohio, too."

Hazel's eyes round. Her mouth opens but no sound comes out. This is way over the line.

My cheeks flush. "Beatrix!"

"And you!" Beatrix cries, turning on me. "Ever since Bee Girl moved to town, you've changed!"

I glance at Hazel and then back to Beatrix. It feels like a teeter-totter moment, but at high speed. I shake my head. "No, I haven't. I'm still the same."

"Not true!" says Beatrix, louder now. "You don't listen to me. You don't act like my friend. If you want to be Hazel's friend so much, go ahead and do it. Because as of right now, we are done! I am not your friend anymore!"

Beatrix shoves her water bottle into her backpack. Hazel is still standing there, holding her tray, mouth gaping.

"Wait," I say to Beatrix. "Don't."

"Just remember," says Beatrix. She's shouting now.

The rest of the cafeteria is perfectly still. "You were the one who told me about how she lied about her dad and the submarine! You thought she was weird, too!"

Beatrix turns and storms out the double doors. Zoe and Arshi grab their things and follow her into the hall.

Hazel's tears are coming now. Not from what Beatrix said, which was mean but expected. But because I am her friend, and she trusted me.

She looks straight at me. "How did you find out about my dad?"

I wince. "I didn't tell her on purpose."

Hazel holds up her hand. "Forget it. I don't want to know."

"I'm sorry," I say. "Let me explain."

I want to tell her everything. I want to say I'm sorry. But before I can say a word, Hazel slams her tray on the table. It echoes in the lunchroom. Everyone is watching.

"I thought you were different," she says. "But you're just like Beatrix." She spins around and storms out of the cafeteria.

Hazel and Beatrix are gone, but it feels like their words are still hanging in the air. I can still hear them in my mind. *Lied about her dad. You were the one who told me. You thought she was weird, too.* And the worst one? *You're just like Beatrix.*

I'm dizzy. I want to hide. If I could, I would back up and have a do-over.

I've lost two friends in one day. And it's all my fault.

ANIMAL FIELDWORK PROJECT

MS. DUPART

EXPLORATORY SCIENCE

SECOND SEMESTER

SIXTH PERIOD

PART

4

Does your subject have a unique way of dealing with extremes?

5 points

Honey bees are very good at dealing with extreme temperatures. They keep the hive temperature stable at around 95 degrees. In the summer, they beat their wings to cool the hive. In winter, they flex their muscles to create warmth. They form a cluster to keep warm. They need one another to survive.

CHAPTER

25

I still feel sick when PE starts. Our class does laps on the track, but Arshi doesn't wait for me like she usually does. I'm not surprised that Arshi is sticking with Beatrix. What's surprising is how much it hurts. And that's not all. The track has a perfect view of the field, so for the entire class, I watch Beatrix and Zoe play softball, laughing and having fun. Later, in science elective, Hazel doesn't speak a word for the entire class—not to me or anyone else.

When the final bell rings, I head straight to the bathroom and hide. I don't want to see Beatrix in the hall. I don't need her to tell me that our carpooling days are over, because I already know. Every Beatrix-and-Meg thing is over.

I walk home by myself and go upstairs to my room. On my bed, I curl on my side and stare out the window. The sun shines, but it feels like it should be raining.

There is a tap on the door. I roll over. "Yes?"

Dad peeks in. "Everything okay?"

"My stomach hurts." It's the truth. The dull ache started sometime during the scene in the lunchroom.

He leans against the doorframe, forehead wrinkling in concern. "Do you want some juice?"

I shake my head. "I want to be by myself."

He shuts the door gently behind him. I'm alone, which is what I wanted. At least, that's what I thought. But now I feel restless. My hands itch to do something. I want to take something apart so I can put it back together. But everything I can think of—my alarm clock, my lamp, my speaker—are all too easy.

After a while, I hear Elsie galloping downstairs. A few minutes later, Mom brings up a tray with flat ginger ale, buttered toast, and canned peaches on the side. Those are my special foods I eat when I'm sick.

Mom studies the tray, frowning faintly. "Sorry, I don't have a bendy straw."

Something catches in my throat. I ball up my fists and push them against my eyes like I can stop my tears, but I can't. They stayed hidden at school, but now that they see the chance, they are coming like they will never stop. My shoulders shake, and before I know it, I'm bawling.

"Hey," Mom says softly. "Hey there. What's wrong? You don't care that much about the straw, do you?"

I shake my head. I *wish* my biggest problem was not having a bendy straw.

Mom sits on the edge of the bed. "Is it your stomach?"

"No," I say. I try to make my breathing slow. "Yes."

"A bit of everything, huh?" Mom asks.

I nod.

Mom's cool fingers trace my forehead. "School stuff?"

"Sort of." It isn't the *most* important thing, but I'm sad that the bee project is ruined. Either because all the bees will be gone or because Hazel will never speak to me again. Or both.

"*Love* stuff?" Mom asks hesitantly.

I wince. "Mom. No."

"Sorry," says Mom, holding up her hands. "Trying to find out what we're dealing with here."

"Okay," I say.

Mom tries again. "Friend stuff?"

I nod, scrubbing at my eyes.

Mom sighs. "Sometimes that's the hardest. Do you want to talk?"

Part of me wants to tell Mom everything, but I don't know where to begin.

"Beatrix and I had an argument," I start.

Mom looks surprised. "But you and Beatrix never fight!"

My teeth find the tender skin on the side of my thumb.

Mom sees what I'm doing and puts her hand on mine. "Don't bite."

I take my thumb from my mouth. I have so much to say, but I don't know where to start. It's like every bit of sadness and anger and frustration is stuck in a giant ball inside me, and there's no way to roll it out.

"Does this have to do with those bees?" Mom frets. "I knew that was going to put you in a bad situation."

This makes me cry harder.

"Oh, sweetie," Mom says, clucking her tongue. "Oh, *sweetie.* What can I get you?"

"Mom," I whisper. "Could you please lie down and hold me for a while?"

I don't have to ask again. She's squeezing alongside me in my bed, not asking questions any longer. She's being just who I need her to be.

CHAPTER
26

Without a best friend, middle school feels like a different planet.

After what happened in the cafeteria, I knew some things would change. Obviously, I won't carpool with Beatrix anymore. But still, I didn't expect to see Zoe and Beatrix strolling into first period with their cups from Uncle Bean's.

It makes my insides ache. Especially when I realize that Zoe's house is out of their way. And that they must have driven right past my house to get to Zoe's. Zoe smiles at me and mouths *hi*, but only when Beatrix isn't looking. In the front row, Hazel stares straight ahead the whole class. I feel like I've been erased.

During math/science block, I can't focus, even though it's our day to present our Pageant of the Planets project. I'm Jupiter, my favorite, but I just stand there glumly, waiting for my moons to stop orbiting so I can read my lines.

At lunch, I skip the cafeteria and head to the library instead. I eat my sandwich among the shelves in the back. It's better than the bathroom, I guess. But after, the food sticks in my stomach in a glob.

For PE, we need partners. I try to catch Arshi's eye, but she turns to Cora instead. The class has an odd number of people, so I have to be partners with Coach Pruett.

By the time science elective starts, I'm exhausted. Hazel is already at our table when I walk in.

"Hi." My voice has a wobble in it, maybe because I've barely talked all day.

Hazel doesn't look up from her paper. My cruddy day gets cruddier.

Ms. Dupart stands at the front of the room. Today her shoes are the color of freshly cut cantaloupe.

"I see that everyone is making lots of progress so far on their packets, so it's time to discuss the final project requirement," she says.

Hazel doesn't budge. I flip open my notebook. I care about the notes, even if Hazel doesn't.

Ms. Dupart writes on the board:

IT'S MORE ART THAN SCIENCE

"Has anyone ever heard this expression? What does it mean?" Ms. Dupart scans the room. "Yes, Warren?"

Warren lowers his hand. "If something is an art, it means there's creativity."

Grace pushes her bangs out of her eyes. "It's saying that science is more logical. It has rules."

Ms. Dupart nods. "I think that is the accepted meaning. But what do you all think? Is *science* more art or more science?"

It almost seems like a trick question.

Parker laughs. "It's science. Science is obviously science."

"Let's take a quick poll," suggests Ms. Dupart. "Raise your hand if you think science is art."

No one raises their hand.

"Raise your hand if you think science is science," says Ms. Dupart.

Now everybody raises their hand—everybody but me. I'm still trying to understand the meaning.

"Meg, I can tell you're thinking hard," says Ms. Dupart. "What are you grappling with?"

Ideas float through my head, but they feel slippery and hard to grasp.

"I think it's both," I say slowly. "The scientific process has rules, and those are important. But before you know the answer, isn't there a lot of guessing? And wondering? That part seems creative in a way, more like art."

Ms. Dupart smiles. "Agreed. Science is both art and science, even though it's not usually described that way. Science requires creativity, and don't let anyone tell you differently."

I have that mixed-up happy-embarrassed feeling from getting a hard question right. I peek at Hazel, who is still looking straight ahead.

"Your presentation must be both informative and creative. Equal points for each. I know many of you feel like the data should stand on their own, but this is a mistake. Data mean nothing without a story that people can understand and relate to."

I like the idea of a story that makes the facts come together.

"I'm passing around handouts that will explain all the details," says Ms. Dupart. "As you are planning, consider the scale of your audience. As much as I love a shoebox diorama, this is not the time or the place. If you stand up at the front of my class with something teeny tiny, you will lose points. Remember, the goal is to engage your audience."

Ms. Dupart hands me two papers. I pass one to Hazel, and she takes it without a word.

"You can use the remainder of class to plan your presentation," Ms. Dupart says. "Use this time wisely."

I read the handout, underlining a few things that seem important. When I finish, I look at Hazel.

"Twenty minutes," Hazel says. "That makes ten for each of us."

I bite my thumb. "We're supposed to work together."

Hazel crosses her arms tightly, like she's hugging herself. "No way. I'm not going to stand up there and do this presentation with you, knowing the whole time you'll be making fun of me behind my back."

Hazel flips her paper over and begins writing. From the corner of my eye, I read the words "interactive Venn diagram" and "population graph."

Everyone around us is talking to their partners. Even Ryan and Alfredo are in deep discussion about their tarantula project. Hazel and I are the only group who isn't speaking to each other.

I want to go back to how things were with Hazel, and it has nothing to do with our grade. I miss her. I wish I knew how to make it right.

CHAPTER

27

I become a master of perfect timing. In first period, I learn to slip into my seat about ten seconds before the morning bell rings, so I don't have to listen to Beatrix and Zoe act like *they* are the ones who've been best friends since kindergarten.

Through total luck, the Fletchers are on vacation, so they don't need us to walk Bart and Lola. I have no idea how Beatrix and I will do that if we aren't speaking to each other next Tuesday.

After literacy block, I vault out of my seat to be one of the first ones out the door. That way, I don't bump into Beatrix or Hazel in the halls. Lunches are almost okay, if

I get to the library early enough to find a spot facing the window. I did have to ask Dad to stop packing celery or chips. I can't get caught eating in the library, or I might be kicked out. I need quiet food.

Science elective has changed forever. Hazel and I sit at the same table, but we might as well be on different planets. We never make eye contact. We never joke about our project or talk about interesting bee facts. I have tried to say I'm sorry, but she ignores me.

Our conversation has been simplified to yes/no questions.

"Are you doing section seven?"

"Yes. Will you do eight and ten?"

"Okay."

I walk around every day with the feeling of something missing. It's worse than forgetting my umbrella or losing my favorite opal necklace from Grandma Lou. It feels like I misplaced a part of myself. I would give anything to find it again.

On Tuesday afternoon, I go to pick up Bart and Lola. I think maybe Beatrix will be there, too, and we will talk and work things out. But Mrs. Fletcher looks confused when I come to the door.

"Beatrix told us you won't have time to walk the dogs anymore," she says. "I sent both the dogs with her."

"That's right," I say. I hate the awkwardness, hate that I'm covering for Beatrix even after all of this. "I forgot."

Every day, I get sadder and sadder. For so long, the biggest force in my life has been Beatrix. In some ways, that bubble of Beatrix's friendship has protected me. In other ways, it has kept me separate from other kids. I've never thought much about making other friends, because I never needed them before.

This, I realize, is what loneliness feels like. I never realized it was possible to say so few words in a day.

On Friday, I stand in the library. I'm eating my sandwich and looking out my favorite window, when I hear something behind me. I'm afraid it's the librarian, but when I turn, I see Arshi peeking around a bookshelf.

"Hey," she says. "I found you."

I'm surprised but happy. "How did you know where to look?"

Arshi glances away. "This is where I went last year when Beatrix was mad at *me*."

I forgot about that. There were a few days in sixth grade—or possibly an entire week—when Beatrix gave Arshi The Freeze. Which meant I gave it, too.

"I don't remember what it was about," I say.

"I wasn't totally sure why," says Arshi. "I was just glad when it was over."

My stomach drops. "I'm so sorry, Arshi."

"Anyway," says Arshi. "That's how I guessed where you were."

"So she's still mad?" I ask, even though I already know.

"Yeah," Arshi says. But then, looking at my face, she adds, "Hopefully she'll forget about it soon."

I don't know about that. A huge fight in the middle of the crowded lunchroom is unforgettable.

I frown. "Where are Beatrix and Zoe?"

"They had a dance meeting," Arshi says. "About their spring performance."

"Oh," I say. This is why she came to find me, I realize. She didn't have anyone to sit with.

Arshi bites her lip. "Don't mention that I was here, okay?"

I feel a pang, even though I understand. She doesn't want Beatrix to know. I wouldn't want to risk The Freeze, either.

"I won't," I say.

"You'll be back with us soon," says Arshi. "Beatrix can't stay mad forever."

I wish that this were true, but something tells me it's not.

That afternoon is one of those spring days that feels as hot as summer. As I walk home, I feel like I'm melting. A mockingbird squawks, chasing a cardinal through the bright blue sky. Mockingbirds are intense. I've seen them attack hawks many times their size—and win.

By the time I get home, my mood is sour. I throw open

the kitchen door. Of course there's nothing decent in the fridge, unless baby carrots or half a container of milk count. Rummaging in the pantry, I locate an almost empty bag of tortilla chips that are mostly crumbs. I take a handful and chew. Stale. It figures.

Dad comes downstairs. "I thought you didn't like chips anymore."

I scowl. "I like chips, but not in my lunch."

Dad blinks slowly, confused.

"They're too noisy at school," I say. "At home, they're fine."

"Okay," says Dad, like it makes perfect sense. "Fantastic."

I crunch another handful of chips.

Dad pours us each a glass of water. "Mom said you're having friend troubles. Something about the bees."

"Beatrix hates me because she thinks I'm on Hazel's side," I say. "Hazel hates me because she thinks I was spying for Beatrix. I have no friends."

"That's rough," says Dad. "Do you think you can fix things?"

"I don't know," I say.

"Do you *want* to fix things?" he asks.

I think for a moment. For Hazel, yes, I would fix it. I shouldn't have shared what I knew about her dad, even though I didn't know Beatrix would use it against Hazel.

It's trickier with Beatrix. I wish she weren't mad at me,

but my feelings about our friendship curve like a question mark.

"Have you ever wanted to keep the good parts of being friends with someone and get rid of the bad?" I ask.

"Definitely," Dad says. "That's how it was with Uncle Joe and me when we were kids."

"What do you mean?" I've never heard about this. I love Uncle Joe, who lives in Seattle and sends me comic books for my birthday.

"I was a goofy, happy-go-lucky kid," says Dad. "And scrawny, with arms like toothpicks. Joe was only a year older but solid."

"And?"

"And he used to pound on me," Dad says. "It was pretty awful at times. The worst part was that I never knew which Joe I was going to get. Fun Joe or Punch in the Stomach Joe."

This is part of the problem with Beatrix, too. I never know who I'm going to get.

"So what did you do?" I ask. "It's not like you could stop being around your brother."

Dad smiles, remembering. "The summer after eighth grade, I grew about six inches. I filled out, too, so I wasn't as scrawny."

That isn't helpful. Even if I were six feet tall, it wouldn't change a thing about how Beatrix and Hazel feel about me.

"But that wasn't what solved it," Dad continues. "Because Joe kept hitting me."

"What happened? Did you punch him back?"

Dad shakes his head. "It was more about how I saw myself. As soon as I stood up to him, he stopped."

That sounds too easy. "Did you guys ever talk about it?"

Dad makes a *hmm* noise. "I guess we never did. Looking back on it, I have some guesses. Our dad was tough on both of us, but especially on Joe. Sometimes he hit Joe pretty hard."

Dad almost never talks about Grandpa Garrison, who died when I was a baby. But in photographs, he always looked stern, with eyebrows in a straight line across his face.

I hate the idea of someone hurting Dad. "But if Uncle Joe knew how it felt to be hit, he should never have done it to you!"

Dad smiles. "True, but that's not always how it works. Especially for kids. It's not always easy to know what's right and wrong if that's what you've been taught at home."

I shake my head. "But you said it was after eighth grade! He was old enough to know better."

"Listen, Meg," Dad says. "I know it feels like you're pretty old right now, but you still have a lot of growing and changing to do. Middle school is a moment. Figuring out who you are is hard. That's your job right now."

I sigh. It's a big job—bigger than I want.

Dad grins at me. "But you know one thing that will never change?"

I roll my eyes because I know what comes next. He's going to tell me that the one thing that will never change is how much he loves me. It's how he wraps up almost every single serious conversation. "What, Dad?"

"How much I love . . . *chips*," he says, grabbing a handful from my bag. "Always have, always will."

It takes me completely by surprise, and I crack up.

He heads for the stairs, crunching his mouthful. "By the way," he says over his shoulder. "These are stale."

I shake my head. "I know that!"

After he leaves, I lean against the kitchen wall. Outside, birds are singing in an obnoxious kind of way. Spring is the loudest season.

Dad believes people can grow and change. It's hard to imagine that being true for Beatrix. I'm not sure that it's true for Hazel, either. They are who they are. I don't think they will change.

But then I think—maybe those words aren't meant for Beatrix or Hazel. Maybe those words are for me.

CHAPTER

28

School is the worst, but Sunday afternoons are almost as bad. Last week, Mom made me go with her to look at new curtains for the living room. I don't want to do that again. I might as well work on my half of the project. I pick up one of my library books and flip pages until I reach my most- and least-favorite page. It's a picture of the inside of the hive. I'm both horrified and fascinated, and I can't look away.

The text on the page explains the way bees control the hive temperature. In the summer, they beat their wings to cool the air. In winter, they gather together and flex their muscles to generate heat.

The idea of all those crawling bees makes my stomach turn. But when I push those feelings aside, I can appreciate how interesting they are. We are going to have to plan our presentation carefully because we only have twenty minutes.

I wonder what she's doing. Probably working on the project, too. Maybe I should go over and see. Nothing is stopping me.

Except one thing. I think I need to tell her I'm sorry. In a way where I really mean it. She'll probably be furious. She may yell at me and say mean things. But I think I need to listen. It's got to be better than silence.

Quickly, before I can change my mind, I tell Mom where I'm going and head out the front door.

The day is warm and humid. By the time I reach Hazel's street, I'm beginning to regret my long-sleeve shirt. As I get closer, I see Hazel sitting on the porch swing. I hesitate for a moment. In my head, I'd imagined knocking on her door. I'm surprised to see her sitting out in the open like this. Even though it's warm, she wears a sweater covered in wildly colored concentric circles.

She looks up and sees me. "What do you want?"

I clear my throat. "I want to say I'm sorry."

Hazel peers over her book. "Would you be saying that if Beatrix were still talking to you?"

"This has nothing to do with her." I can hear my voice shake, which I hate. It makes me sound like I'm not sure.

Hazel glares. Clearly, she doesn't believe me. "You acted like a spy for her. I bet you were the one who told her we were moving our bees. And the stuff about my dad—that's none of your business."

Shame squeezes my ribs, works its way around my throat. I don't know how to answer. I bite my thumb instead.

"You don't have anything to say now," Hazel says. "I wish I'd known that the girls in this town are so mean. I want to go back to Newford. At least the kids are nicer there."

Even if Hazel says the kids were nicer there, I know the truth. Hazel doesn't have any kid friends in Newford. She must be super unhappy if she wants to go back. It's Beatrix's fault. Why does she have to be so mean?

I open my mouth to say the words, but something stops me. Putting the blame on Beatrix is easy. She did some nasty things. She was meaner and nastier than I thought was possible. She gave Hazel lots of reasons to be unhappy.

But if I'm being honest, there's another person who could have been kinder. Who could have done things differently.

There's a lump in my throat. I swallow hard but it stays put.

For a long time now, I've been a part of Beatrix-and-Meg. Beatrix was strong and I was weak. Beatrix was harsh and I was sweet.

If Beatrix were here, she'd say, "Go ahead, Hazel. Go

back to Newford. Your mom says you don't have any friends there anyway."

But Beatrix isn't here, and Beatrix-and-Meg no longer exists. For the first time in what feels like forever, it doesn't matter what Beatrix says. What matters is what I say.

"I'm sorry," I say. "I said some things I shouldn't have to Beatrix. I wish I'd been a better friend to you. A real friend, not a sometimes-friend."

Hazel's fierceness wavers a bit. Not all the way. But it's something.

"Prove it," she says.

"Okay," I say. "How?"

We are quiet. It's a teeter-totter moment. Will we go back to not talking or will we be friends for real?

Hazel thinks for a long time. I stand there, waiting. I want to chew my thumb, but I squeeze it instead. Eventually her eyes light up and a slow grin spreads across her face. Her expression is friendly and wide open. I think back to that day in Beatrix's driveway, when I bumped into Hazel and the grape jelly meatballs crashed to the ground. So much has happened since then, good and bad. I don't know how to make it better, but from the way Hazel is smiling, I think maybe she does.

I grin back.

Fifteen minutes later, I've pulled on a bee suit over my clothes.

I can't believe I'm going to get up close with the bees. My heart is beating fast, so I try to focus on the way the suit feels. I hate this. But I want to show Hazel that I am serious about saving the bees. I am serious about being her friend.

"So weird," I say, stretching out my arms. "I feel like I'm going to outer space."

"You look like it," Hazel says, grinning.

The only thing I need help with is a pair of straps with hook-and-loop fasteners. "How do I use these?"

"Those go around the bottom of the coveralls, so you won't get bees in your pants," Hazel says, smirking.

I shudder. The idea of a single bee is bad enough, but the idea of *thousands* of bees trapped inside my coveralls is almost enough to make me run out the front door screaming. But I'm staying put. I can tell Hazel thinks I don't have the guts to do it. I fasten the straps so tight, even a single larva couldn't pass through.

In the yard, Hazel uses the smoker to calm the bees before opening the hive.

"I wanted to show you all this stuff up close," Hazel says excitedly. "The honeycomb—see how yellow and waxy it is? It's delicious. It melts if you spread it on warm buttered toast."

I'm about to tell her that the idea is absolutely disgusting, but then I look at the frame she's holding. Immediately, I feel sick to my stomach. I tell myself to look at the flowers, the sky, the trees—anything but the fifty thousand bees crawling inside the hive.

"Interesting," I manage to squeak out. I find an interesting cloud and stare at it.

The bees can't hurt me, as long as I am wearing the suit. I'm safe, I'm safe, I'm safe. A few fly toward me and bounce off my suit. They buzz loudly. Panic rises inside me.

I wave at one by my ear. "They seem to, um, not like me very much."

"Don't wave at them," Hazel says automatically. I know from my reading that waving at them might make them more upset. "They seem irritated today."

Great. Of all the days to see the bees, I picked a time when they're in a bad mood.

"If you're afraid, you can always go back inside." Hazel turns her back to me.

For a minute, I'm tempted. Each time I glance away from my cloud, a fresh wave of anxiety washes over me. I want to prove something to Hazel. But I'm starting to think that maybe I *need* to prove something to myself.

"It's not so bad," I lie.

Hazel disassembles the hive and checks the comb. She is quiet, methodical. She keeps looking at the same frame again and again, holding it up to the light. It seems like it's

taking a longer time than usual. I'm about to say something to that effect when Hazel turns to me.

"I don't see any eggs," Hazel says.

I squint at her. That doesn't seem right. A queen lays
one or two thousand eggs a day. "Are you sure?"

"Meg, I'm positive!" Hazel exclaims. Fear and panic
mix together in her voice. "I can't find the queen. She's
missing . . . or dead."

"Maybe she's hiding." I risk a peek, but when I see the
frame crawling with bees, my stomach lurches.

"Even if I manage to find her, she isn't laying," she says.
"That means she's in trouble. I need to talk to Claudia
now."

She reassembles the hive quickly, like a puzzle she
knows by heart.

When we go inside, she disappears down the hall,
probably going to call Claudia.

I struggle to unfasten the bee suit. I wish I under-
stood more about what was happening. Even with all my
research, I feel unprepared. I know that sometimes worker
bees make emergency queen cells, where the queen lays
eggs that can be made into queens. But that works only
if the cell is made while the queen is alive and laying.
Otherwise, the whole hive could be lost.

Finally, Hazel returns holding a tablet in one hand.
She's pale but less panicked than before.

"She thinks I probably caught it in time. She is going

to check with other beekeepers to see if they have a queen for my hive."

"That's good," I say. "It will be okay."

Hazel shakes her head. "I have been so distracted with everything that I almost skipped checking the hive. What if I had? They need me, and I almost let them down."

I look at my watch. "Is your mom at yoga?"

Hazel bites her lip. "She's on a work trip. I said I would be okay by myself. But this stinks. I wish she were here."

The tablet chimes and Hazel looks at it, wiping her eyes. "Claudia says she found a queen for me. She'll pick it up, and then she'll be on her way."

"Good," I say.

She hesitates. "You can go. If you want."

I shake my head. "I'll wait."

Hazel looks relieved. "All right. But it doesn't mean everything is okay with us."

"Got it," I say.

I sit at the kitchen table. For more than an hour, Hazel travels between the kitchen window, where she looks for her bees, and her front door, where she looks for Claudia. Finally a dusty pickup truck pulls into the driveway.

Claudia steps out of the truck. She's younger than Astrid, maybe my mom's age. Her hair is dark and wavy and hangs down her back. Her round brown eyes light up when she sees Hazel barreling in her direction. She gives Hazel a big hug. Hazel starts to cry, but Claudia shushes her.

"It's going to be okay," Claudia says. I like her already.

Hazel helps unload the truck. When Claudia comes up to the front porch, I can see that her cardigan sweater has elephants on the pockets. I smile. I think I've found the source of Hazel's sweaters.

She stretches out her hand to shake mine.

"Claudia Castillo," she says, looking at me appraisingly.

"I'm Meg," I say.

"I know," Claudia says. There's a look in her eye that makes me feel like Hazel has told her everything.

They both go inside, leaving me on the porch. I realize that I could leave now. But I said I would stick with Hazel, and I meant it. Besides, the scientist in me wants to see the part that happens next.

Claudia sets a bin on the kitchen table, then removes a small box. It's made of plastic and is covered with air holes. "Here she is."

I can see at least three bees inside.

"She's with her attendants," says Hazel. "To keep her fed and happy."

"You already know that pheromones send important messages to all the members of the hive," Claudia says. "If we force a new queen on an established colony, they would kill her."

"Because they wouldn't recognize her pheromones," Hazel adds.

Claudia points to the end of the box, where a short tube extends. "This is candy. Over the next few days, it will be eaten away by the worker bees. This allows a slow introduction. The colony can see and smell the queen, but they can't hurt her. By the time the candy has been eaten away, they will accept her as one of their own."

I have to admit that it's a smart system.

"At least, that's how it works, ideally. Sometimes it's not quite so easy," says Claudia. "But we'll see. Why don't you girls suit up, and we'll go see what we are dealing with?"

"Oh, no," I say, holding back a shudder. I don't want to get that close.

"Come on, Meg," Hazel says.

I cringe. "I don't think so."

Hazel shrugs. I can tell she's disappointed.

"No big deal," she says stiffly. She's acting like it doesn't bother her, but I know I hurt her feelings.

I want them to see that I can do it. I need them to know that the bees are important to me, and that *Hazel* is important to me, too.

"All right," I say. "I'll do it."

The three of us suit up and head outside.

"The bees seemed irritated before," Hazel warns.

Claudia nods. "That's common with queenless hives. Her presence keeps them steady. Without her, they get a little feisty."

The waves of anxiety from before are flooding me

now. I tell myself to breathe, thinking of the model lung in Ms. Dupart's classroom. I breathe in, imagine the alveoli in my lung like little balloons. In and out, in and out, breathe, breathe, breathe.

Meanwhile, Claudia and Hazel disassemble the hive. They work perfectly together. Claudia inspects the combs and confirms that there are no eggs. She can't find the queen, either. I make the mistake of looking straight into the hive, which gives me a perfect view of thousands of crawling worker bees squeezing past one another. I look away and try to fan myself. I'm starting to feel hot underneath the beekeeping gear.

"These are brood combs," Claudia explains. "Where the eggs are laid and the babies are kept. I don't see any eggs, so that means it's been a few days since the queen has been around. I'm checking carefully for queen cups, to see if the colony has started a new queen. But I'm not seeing any, which means they may be more willing to accept the one I brought."

Claudia picks up the plastic box with the queen and her attendants, then places it on top of the frames. Worker bees gather on the cage, trying to get close to the new guest.

"They're surrounding her," I say. I wonder if I'm breathing in and out too deeply, because I'm starting to feel dizzy. It's hot in this bee suit.

"This is a good sign," Claudia says, pointing at them. "They're curious. See how they fan her with their wings?"

Claudia gently brushes at the cluster of bees. They separate easily from the little box. "If they weren't going to accept her, they would cling tightly, almost creating a ball around her. They'd be pointing their bottoms into the cage."

I'm feeling weird, kind of sick to my stomach. After this is over, I might want to lie down.

"Why would they do that?" I ask. "With their bottoms?"

Claudia looks at me in surprise. "So they can kill her, of course."

The words echo in my mind. If the colony doesn't accept the queen, she will be destroyed.

I don't feel so good, I think to myself. Or maybe I say it out loud, because Claudia's and Hazel's faces are turning toward me. Even behind their veils, I can see they look worried.

It's the last thing I remember before everything goes dark.

CHAPTER
29

I'm lying in the grass, flat on my back. Hazel hovers a few inches from my face, staring at me through my veil.

"What happened?" I ask.

"You fainted," says Claudia.

"Oh." I remember now. The signs were all there, but I didn't realize what it was. I've been so worried about fainting, but when it was actually happening, I didn't even notice. The thought makes me giggle.

"What?" Hazel asks. "Why are you laughing? Are you okay? Did you get stung?"

I try to sit up, but I'm not quite ready.

"Stay there a bit longer," Claudia advises. "Then we'll go inside and get you a drink of juice."

She reassembles the hive in an efficient yet unhurried way. Hazel stays right by me.

"I didn't get stung," I say. "I have this fainting thing that sometimes happens when I get nervous."

"You do? I didn't know you were *that* scared of bees," Hazel says. She almost sounds mad at me.

"I told you that I'm terrified of them," I say. "What did you think that meant?"

"I didn't know it meant you might faint!" Hazel says. "I tried to take your pulse. I was about to call an ambulance. Why did you come out here with the bees if you're so afraid?"

"I wanted you to know I'm serious," I say. "That I'm not a spy."

"No harm done," says Claudia. "Come on, Hazel, support her on the other side, and we will help walk her in."

Together we go inside, moving slowly. Hazel helps me take off the bee suit, and I sink into the squishy couch in the living room. Hazel and Astrid still haven't unpacked all the boxes, but now they feel like part of the room to me.

Hazel brings me cranberry juice in a jelly jar and watches me drink it.

"I'm going to make you a snack," Claudia says. "Can you give me your parents' number? I think I should give them a call."

I tell her the number. Claudia dials while opening cabinets and drawers.

"Are you sure you're okay?" Hazel asks. "I thought something really bad had happened."

"I used to faint all the time, when I was little," I say. "I'd get anxious and pass out."

Claudia returns from the kitchen with plates of sliced cheddar and sprouted-grain crackers. After I eat, I start to feel more normal. It's like I'm coming back to my body.

"Thanks for helping me, both of you," says Hazel. "I didn't want them to die, even if I don't get to keep them past Thursday."

"Thursday?" I ask. "What happens Thursday?"

"Town council meeting," Hazel says. "They allow public comment, so I'm going to go and talk about why they should let me keep my bees."

"But that's so soon," I say. "Are you ready?"

Hazel shrugs. "I've made some notes. I'm going to fight for them, even if it won't do any good."

I see Mom's car pull up to Hazel's house. Claudia lets her in.

"Are you all right?" Mom asks in a rush. She puts her hand on my forehead.

"I don't have a fever, Mom. I just fainted," I say.

"Are you okay to walk to the car?" Mom asks.

"I'm fine," I say. I stand up. "Nice to meet you, Claudia. Thanks for the snack."

"Hope to see you again," says Claudia.

I turn to Hazel. "I can come over tomorrow after school if you want. To help you get ready for the meeting."

Hazel brightens. "I'd like that."

Maybe things aren't all the way back to normal, but it feels like a step in the right direction.

Mom walks me to the passenger side of the car and waits for me to get in. When I do, she reaches over like she's going to fasten my seat belt.

I am mortified. "Mom, no! I can do it myself."

"All right, all right," Mom says. "I worry, that's all."

She gets in the car. The drive back to the house is short and quiet. Soon Mom is pulling into our garage. I start to open the door, but she stops me.

"Wait," Mom says. "I don't like all this business with the bees. I'm so worried to see your anxiety back. You haven't fainted in so long."

I shake my head. "Mom, it's not a big deal. I do get nervous around the bees, but being friends with Hazel is more important than me being nervous."

Mom frowns. "You should never have put yourself in danger, Meg."

"I wanted to prove something to Hazel—" I say.

But Mom is interrupting. "A friend should never make you feel like you have to prove yourself. Think about your friendship with Beatrix—she accepts you as you are. She's never made you so nervous that you fainted."

Anger sparks inside me. She's talking about a different version of Beatrix, not the one I know now.

"Sure, she never made me nervous back in *kindergarten*," I say. "Trust me, Beatrix makes me nervous now. She won't even talk to me."

Mom frowns. "But Mrs. Bailey said that Hazel is the one causing problems."

Of course Mrs. Bailey stuck her nose in where it doesn't belong. "She doesn't know everything."

The corners of Mom's mouth turn down. "I don't know what to do, Meg. I have no idea what's going on with you and Beatrix. You won't open up about it. Ever since that day you came home crying, you've been miserable."

I feel like I have a boulder inside me, squeezing on my heart and stomach. There is so much Mom doesn't know. I need to try to tell her.

"Something changed last year with Beatrix," I say. "If I make her mad, she drops me for a while. And it feels awful. After that, I had to watch myself constantly so I didn't say or do anything to make her angry. I used to think I could be careful enough to be her friend. But I don't know if I can keep doing it."

Mom still looks puzzled. "She may have a strong personality, but she adores you, Meg. Her family, too. Mrs. Bailey sounds so sad that you haven't been around."

I sigh. "The Baileys might look perfect on the outside,

but they're not on the inside. Mrs. Bailey is sometimes really, really not nice."

Gnawing my thumb, I try to think of the right way to say the next part. I don't want to hurt Mom, but I feel like I need to tell her.

"Remember that party in January, when she asked you to make those grape jelly meatballs? She didn't even serve them."

Mom doesn't answer. Maybe I hurt her feelings. Or maybe she's shocked.

But when I look at her, she doesn't look surprised at all. She sighs and leans back against her seat.

"Mom?" I ask. "What is it? Did you hear me?"

Mom nods. "I know about the meatballs. It's not the first time she's done it."

My mouth gapes open. "But, Mom! You *knew*? Doesn't that make you mad?"

Mom sighs. "It used to. And it hurt my feelings, too."

"It's so rude of her," I say. "Why does she do it?"

Mom shrugs. "I don't know why. Maybe it makes her feel better about her fancy caterers. Maybe she feeds them to her family the next night . . . or to her dogs."

"You should tell her you can't make them anymore," I say.

"I don't know if it's worth it," Mom says. "It's such a small thing for me to do. If Mrs. Bailey has these parties for the whole neighborhood, volunteers constantly at school, and takes you on trips to their fabulous beach house . . . well, I guess I can manage a batch of my meatballs if she asks. It doesn't matter what she chooses to do with them."

I'm squeezing my fists so tight, I can feel my fingernails pushing into my palms.

"It matters," I say. "If you don't say no, she'll keep asking for every party, and you'll be making meatballs forever! You shouldn't go along with her because it makes things easier."

"Oh, sweetie." Mom reaches out to me, but I pull back. I've never been so mad at her.

"Beatrix is your friend, and her family is lovely to you. Is it really that hard to choose to get along with them? To choose a friend over something that doesn't mean anything, in the long run?"

I don't want to listen anymore. It sounds like Mom is saying she couldn't stand up for herself because of my friendship with Beatrix. That somehow it's my fault that she's been making meatballs all these years. I never asked her to do that.

"The bees matter to Hazel," I say. "And they matter to me. And if Beatrix won't be my friend because of the bees, then I think that's Beatrix's problem. Not mine."

My heart is pounding, and I feel like I could scream. When I go inside the house, Elsie runs up to me, purse swinging.

"Hi! Hi, Meg. Let's play tigers!"

"Not now, Elsie," I say. My voice comes out much harsher than I mean it to.

She jumps in surprise. Her huge blue eyes shimmer for a moment before the tears start to fall. The sound of my little sister crying makes my heart pinch, but I can't handle Elsie right now. I need to be in my room.

As I climb the stairs, I hear Dad pick up Elsie and soothe her. I feel more alone than ever.

CHAPTER
30

Mom and I are avoiding each other again. We don't say much to each other that evening. Monday morning, she leaves for work before I wake up. But no matter what she thinks, I'm going to stick with my plan to help Hazel.

After school I drop off my things at home and go straight to Hazel's. Books, papers, highlighters, and pens are already spread across the kitchen table.

"First, I thought we should outline my speech," Hazel says. "Unless you want to make a speech, too?"

I feel bad disappointing her, but I have my limits.

"I hate public speaking," I say.

"That's okay," says Hazel. "You can help make a giant poster with all the data. I saw a graph that I want to include, too." She picks up a highlighter and goes back to marking a section in one of the books.

I pause. Something doesn't feel right. With Beatrix, if something bothered me, I would just push it to the side. But I don't want to do that anymore. Friends should talk to each other when there's a problem.

"Hazel," I say. "Can we talk about something first? It's important."

Hazel's eyebrows pinch in distracted concern, but she doesn't look up. "Do you think we need more books? If so, we could go to the library."

I shake my head. "I want to ask you about something I don't understand."

Hazel uses her finger to mark her place in the book and then looks at me. "Okay. Go for it."

I take a deep breath. Instead of biting my thumb, I squeeze it.

"Why did you say that stuff about your dad being on the submarine if it wasn't true?"

Hazel closes her eyes. She's quiet for a while, like she's thinking hard. I feel bad for bringing it up. But I want to see inside. I want to understand.

Finally, she opens her eyes.

"My dad hasn't ever been around much," she says. "He and Astrid split up right after I was born. She says it's not my fault, but . . ."

Hazel shrugs.

"I don't think he exactly *wanted* a kid," she finishes.

I try not to look shocked. I think of my own dad and what it might be like if he felt that way. When Hazel sees me, she shakes her head firmly.

"Don't feel sorry for me," she says. "It's just how he is."

"Okay," I say.

"Anyway, I do see him sometimes," she continues. "Like for an afternoon, once in a while. About two years ago, we watched a nature documentary about octopuses. Then, just before we moved, I learned about the *Haliphron atlanticus*. I wrote him a letter about it. He was excited—he wrote back and everything."

She clears her throat. "It may sound stupid, but sometimes I take little pieces of what I know about him and kind of make up a story. I've done it ever since I was really small. It makes me feel more connected to him."

I think I understand why she would imagine. But when she told us about it, that story became a lie. That's the part I don't get.

"That day at Beatrix's house, she hated me right away. I don't know why," Hazel continues. "She has a perfect family and a giant house. When she started asking about my dad, I didn't know how to explain that he moved all the way to Ohio—that I didn't know when I'd see him again. All I knew was that I didn't want to give her another thing to be mean about."

I think of Beatrix that day. She was so angry. It surprised me, too.

Hazel shakes her head. "Obviously, that didn't work. I should have just told the truth."

"I don't know if it would have made any difference," I say.

"Maybe not." Hazel sighs, looking out the window. "I don't expect you to understand. Your family is pretty perfect, too. But if you want to know why I said it, that's the answer."

I have a lot to think about.

First, I think about Hazel's dad. He is missing out on an exceptionally interesting person.

I think about Beatrix. We never talked like this. Maybe if we had, things would be different.

Then I think of Mom and feel a little jolt. She and I don't talk like this, either. I know she wants what's best for me, but she doesn't always know what that is. Especially if I don't tell her what's really been happening in my life. My family isn't perfect, but I know they love me.

I don't know exactly what it feels like to be in Hazel's shoes. But I know what it feels like to want something else from someone—to want something more than they can give.

"Thanks," I say.

Hazel looks at me. "For what?"

"For telling me."

She smiles. "Thank you. For asking."

We smile at each other and then get to work.

CHAPTER
31

It's the day before the town council meeting, and we're at our regular spots at Hazel's kitchen table. Over the past three days, we've worked for hours, but it doesn't seem like we're ready.

Hazel groans in frustration. "Three minutes isn't nearly enough time. I wish I could speak longer."

She shoves the stack of papers across the table. "How am I going to get through all this material?"

I look at the pages. Hazel is right—there's no way to get all this information into a three-minute presentation. If she tries to cover everything, it will take a whole hour.

"Let's work on the poster," I suggest. "Something eye-catching, with a picture."

Hazel looks happy to focus on something new. "That's a great idea! I'll get the stuff."

When she returns with the paper and supplies, we get started. I'm good at bubble letters, so I use a marker to write Save the Bees on the poster board. Together we color in the letters. I like helping Hazel. I'm also glad it's behind the scenes. I don't like to give speeches. It's one thing to do a presentation in Ms. Dupart's class, but the idea of speaking in front of a big town council meeting makes my stomach clench. Hazel is worried about three minutes being too short, but to me, three minutes would feel like an eternity.

Hazel taps her chin, deep in thought. "We have to fit a lot of graphs on this thing."

I look at her sideways. "Maybe one, right? No more than that."

"Nope," Hazel says. "We'll use every inch. The more data, the better."

I cap my marker. "Hazel, no. If you put too much on the poster, no one will read it."

Hazel frowns. "I want it to be accurate."

"Try to make it look nice," I say. "Not too crowded. Remember, science and art together, like Ms. Dupart said."

"Hmm," Hazel says. She's listening, but I don't know if she's convinced. "I want to practice my speech again. Will you time me?"

I get my timer ready and Hazel starts.

"Hi, I'm Hazel, and I want to talk to you about bees.

Did you know that honey bees in the United States face many challenges? Partly due to parasites, lack of food for the bees, and even environmental stressors and accidental pesticide exposure."

She's speaking quickly. I know she's worried about getting all the facts in, but I hope she will slow down when she speaks at the meeting. It's too hard to understand otherwise.

Hazel points to a graph in one of the books. "This is about colony collapse disorder. It has to do with the worker bees leaving the hive, which leaves the queen behind with lots of young bees but not enough to do the jobs the older bees do. This has caused a dramatic effect on honey bees, and the population may never recover."

Hazel continues to refer to her graphs and data. It's important information, but she's talking so fast, it's hard to follow—even for me, and I already know a lot of the facts, because of our project.

"Um," Hazel says, pointing to a picture in one of the articles. "This shows that honey bees are important for pollinating fruits and vegetables. Okra, kiwi, celery, strawberries . . ."

When she finally finishes, she asks me how long it was.

"Um," I say. "Twelve minutes."

Hazel's shoulders slump. "Twelve minutes? But I'll only have three at the meeting. I'll never squeeze it all in."

"It was not awful," I say. "That was an amazing amount of bee facts."

I pause.

Hazel looks at me. *"And?"*

"It was too much," I say. "Even if you shorten it, it will still feel like a wall of facts. And remember, I already know most of what you're talking about. On Thursday night, this information will be new for the council. If you give a speech like this, they might not understand any of it."

Hazel rubs at her eyelids. "I wish I knew what to do."

"Maybe just take one angle," I say. "So if you want to concentrate on how bees help the environment, you could talk about how they pollinate plants. And maybe we could draw a cute bee on the poster, too."

Hazel's forehead wrinkles. "A *cute* bee?"

"Remember what Ms. Dupart says," I say. "Science is art."

I can tell she's not convinced, but she lets me draw a bee on the poster anyway. I make sure she has a big smile, and I don't add the stinger. Maybe Hazel will listen to me and make her speech a bit shorter. I hope so.

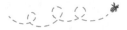

On the day of the meeting, I go straight home and work on homework. Hazel said she has a dentist appointment, so she and Astrid will meet me there.

"Do you need a ride over?" Dad asks.

"I think I'll walk," I say. "Hazel and Astrid will probably give me a ride home after."

Hazel and I have been inside working so much that it's nice to feel the sunshine. I see a bee visiting a flower and hope it's one of Hazel's.

Town Hall is a squat brick building with white columns and stone steps. Dad says that it's trying to look grander than it is, but I think it looks solid and impressive. When I walk up the steps, my insides flutter. I'm nervous enough with this small building. I can't imagine how I'd feel if it were bigger. I have to stick my hands in my pockets so I don't chew my thumbs.

Inside is a small table, staffed by a man with a shiny bald head and a thick mustache. He has two clipboards.

"Sign in on the visitor list with your name and address," he says, pointing at a yellow paper. "Are you speaking at the meeting?"

He doesn't wait for an answer. Instead, he taps the second clipboard.

"If you want to speak, you need to sign up on this green sheet. Only ten speakers are allowed at each meeting, three minutes per speaker."

I glance at the list. Half the speaker spots are already taken. Mrs. Bailey's name is there in neat cursive. Hazel hasn't arrived yet.

"Definitely not speaking," I say. "Here for a friend."

After I sign in on the yellow sheet, I head into the meeting room. The front of the room is already full of people, but there are spaces in the back. Beatrix and Mrs. Bailey sit in the front row, Rocco perched on Beatrix's lap. They are surrounded by neighbors, including Zoe and her mom. Each person is wearing a little pin that says Bee Afraid. I have to admit, that is kind of clever.

As I'm checking out the pins, I accidentally make eye contact with Beatrix. But when Beatrix sees me, she looks away. She whispers something to Zoe, and they start to giggle.

My face burns. I slink to an empty row in the back. Being here feels like a mistake. I don't know where Hazel is. If she doesn't show up by the time the meeting starts, I'm sneaking out.

The minutes click by, and the room continues to fill up. Several people stop to talk to Mrs. Bailey on the way in. She is handing out pins. If I hadn't known before, it would be obvious now that Mrs. Bailey knows the whole town. It feels like the entire room is wearing one of those pins. Everyone but me.

I give up and chew on my thumb a bit. Seeing everyone wear those pins is discouraging. It feels like the whole thing has been decided already, before the meeting even starts. I turn sideways in my seat, looking at the pictures of past mayors, who are mostly old men with skin the same color as mine. Their ties change, but other than that, they all look the same.

Someone is in the aisle with me, probably needing to pass. But when I look up, it's Mom, still in her work clothes.

"M-Mom," I stammer. "What are you doing here?"

She's smiling. "Can I sit with you?"

I can't manage to speak, but I make myself nod.

Mom sits down and smooths her clothes.

"I've been thinking about our talk," Mom says. "And I realized something. The most important kind of loyalty is not to a friend, or a town, or anything else. The best, most important kind of loyalty can be the hardest. But it's what you've been trying to do this whole time."

I shake my head. "I don't understand."

Mom's smile is a swirl of both happy and sad. She reaches over and tucks a strand of hair behind my ear.

"The very most important kind of loyalty is when you manage to be loyal to yourself," she says. "Especially when others are telling you not to. And that's what you've done. Even when I told you not to, you listened to yourself about the bees and about your friendships."

Mom is looking at me with an expression that is so warm, I have to glance away. It feels like looking at the sun.

"I thought about what you said in the car," Mom says.

"And?" I ask.

"And," she says quietly, "I am so very proud of you."

"For what?"

"For trying to do the right thing," she says. "Even when it's hard."

"Thanks." My voice is scratchy all of a sudden.

Mom pats my hand. At the front of the room, there is

a stir of activity. Several of the council members file in. One recognizes Mrs. Bailey and waves hello.

I look around wildly. I don't see Hazel.

"Mom," I whisper. "Hazel's not here yet. What if she doesn't get a chance to speak?"

Mom's glance travels around the room. "Are you sure she's coming? Go see if she's on her way in."

I stand up and make my way to the lobby. I don't see Hazel. Where could she be?

I look at the mustachioed staff member at the little table.

"Can I sign someone up on the speaker list who isn't here yet? I know she'll be here soon."

He shakes his head from side to side. "No can do. The rules say that speakers must sign themselves in."

I frown, thinking. Then I know what to do.

I take a pen from the table. My hand wobbles as I write it, but I manage to scratch my name on the pale green sheet. If Hazel doesn't arrive, I will speak in her place. Even if the idea makes me want to faint right here on the fake-marble floor of the Willow Pond Town Hall.

CHAPTER

32

When I return, there are eight minutes until the meeting is supposed to begin. I slip in next to Mom. I can't believe I signed up on the green sheet. I lean over to Mom and ask for a pen and paper. I hope Hazel gets here soon, but in case she doesn't, I should make some notes about what to say.

Mom hands me a small notebook and a ballpoint pen. I try to concentrate on making the best bee speech I can, but all I can think about is the entire room staring at me, especially Beatrix. The idea makes my words dry up.

An officer stands at the front of the room. "We're about to call the meeting to order. Everyone, please find your seats."

My eyes are glued to the doorway. Where is Hazel?

At the front of the room, the council members are finding their places. Their seats are large and padded, with armrests, not like the metal folding chair I'm sitting on.

Mayor Pierce, who sits in the middle of the semicircle, shuffles a few papers in front of her. Her nose is very, very narrow, and then it flares at the bottom.

"We usually don't get such attendance at our meetings," she says. "I can only imagine this is regarding the concern about the bees?"

"That's right," someone calls out from the front row.

"Very well," says Mayor Pierce. "The meeting is called to order."

I grab Mom's arm. "Oh no! It's too late. Hazel can't sign up to speak."

Mom's forehead scrunches in a worried way. She pats my hand, but there's nothing she can do. I look at my scribbled notes, but that was the backup plan. I didn't think I'd really have to do it.

"First we will discuss old business," says the mayor.

The minutes of the old meeting are read and then voted on. Then a few announcements about things that have already happened. And then even *more* announcements, this time about things that will happen later, like an arts festival downtown in June. Then there are even more announcements about what is happening in Willow Pond's sister cities, which apparently there are six of.

I know one thing for sure: I'll never run for town council. Meetings are boring.

The door swings wide and Hazel bursts in. She carries a poster that's almost as big as she is, every inch covered with graphs and tables. Astrid follows, and Claudia is with her. And behind them is Ms. Dupart! It's a shock to see her outside of school, and my mouth falls open. When Ms. Dupart sees me, I get a tiny wink and a smile. She's wearing bright-yellow high heels. I think it's for luck, for the bees.

The group squeezes past the chairs and into my row. Hazel plops down next to me.

"We got a flat tire! Claudia had to come get us." She looks like she's going to cry. "I didn't get a chance to sign up. I'm going to lose my bees."

"Hazel," I say. "I signed up to speak."

Her eyes widen. "You did?"

I nod, trying to hide the feeling that my stomach is trying to crawl out of my throat.

She digs in her pocket and hands me a folded square of paper. "Here's my speech, if you want to use it. And don't forget the poster."

Up close, I can see that it is jam-packed with facts, graphs, charts, and even a map of our neighborhood. It makes me smile when I see she tried to balance out the data with a few cartoon bees she drew in herself. She even glued googly eyes on them.

"Nice," I say.

Hazel grins. "Thanks. I hope it works."

"Me too," I say.

Finally, it is time for the speaker portion to begin.

"We are ready for our first speaker," says Mayor Pierce into a microphone. "Olivia Kobayashi is our first speaker."

Ms. Kobayashi adjusts the microphone until it is at the right height. She wants a traffic light added to the intersection of Third Avenue and Elm Street to make it safer for pedestrians.

Then one of Mrs. Bailey's friends speaks, Kendra Wallace.

"I don't think people should be allowed to keep bees in our town, because they can sting children. Or pets," she adds, glancing at Mrs. Bailey, who nods. "It is wrong for one neighbor to make choices for an entire neighborhood. No one should have more rights than others."

Another one of Mrs. Bailey's friends speaks and repeats almost the same things as Mrs. Wallace, except arranged in a different order. As she speaks, it becomes clear that she and Mrs. Bailey work at the same real estate office. Also, she lets it slip that she lives two towns over. Which is not exactly fair, when you realize she doesn't live anywhere near the bees. I look at Hazel and can tell she agrees with me.

Next up is Mr. Shaw, the grump who lives on the corner where my street intersects with Beatrix's. He is legendary for his crankiness and loves to yell at people when they don't do what he wants. I grimace. This is not going to be good.

"I want to talk about the bees," he says in his creaky old voice. This is classic Mr. Shaw. I sigh.

"I don't like bees," he continues. "And do you know something else? I don't like barking dogs, either. Some people in this room have dogs that bark all day long." He cranes his neck and looks pointedly at Mrs. Bailey.

I raise my eyebrows at Hazel. Maybe this is going to be good.

"But that doesn't mean that anyone should get rid of their bees. Or that people should get rid of their dogs. Unless the owners can't keep their dogs from doing their business on my yard, in which case people *should* get rid of those dogs."

A few people on the council chuckle. Mr. Shaw doesn't crack a smile. He would never joke about his lawn.

"The point of living in a neighborhood is that we all have things we don't like, and we have to get by. This Hazel is a nice girl. She should be allowed to keep her bees. That's it."

He finishes abruptly and goes back to his seat. I stare at Hazel, who smiles shyly.

"Wow! What did you do?" I ask. "Mr. Shaw doesn't like anything. Or anyone."

"I gave him some of the honey left from last season," she says. "I guess he liked it."

"That honey is magic," I say, and Hazel grins.

Now another friend of Mrs. Bailey's is speaking. It's the same message as the others—bees are not good for kids or animals. It's untrue and also boring to hear the same thoughts again and again.

A man speaks about needing accessible swings at the Cedar Bend playground. Then Mrs. Bailey's name is called. She walks to the front. In one hand, she clutches a stack of notecards. In the other arm, she carries Rocco, who wears a tiny hat topped with a pom-pom.

He is adorable.

Unfairly adorable.

This is when I know for sure that we are in real trouble.

CHAPTER
33

"Aww," say several of the members of the audience, one council member, and *Hazel*.

"Hazel," I whisper. "Shh!"

"You have to admit," she says under her breath. "He is adorable."

"I'm here to talk about the danger of beekeeping within a neighborhood," Mrs. Bailey says smoothly. "I implore the council to recognize that our part of Willow Pond is residential, with many homes in close proximity. A rural community would be more appropriate for bee farm activities."

Hazel doesn't have a *farm*. Mrs. Bailey is saying that to

make it sound like keeping a beehive is something that belongs out in the country. But bees can live almost anywhere, even in a city. They don't need farmland.

"Last month, my sweet dog Rocco was attacked by my neighbor's vicious bees." Mrs. Bailey squeezes Rocco close. Beatrix holds a sign in the air. It shows a large photograph of Rocco dressed up as a dinosaur.

"Aww!" says Hazel. "A triceratops. How cute."

I frown at her.

"I'm sorry," Hazel whispers. "But it's such a cute costume."

I sigh. In a cuteness contest, dogs beat bees every time.

Mrs. Bailey continues. "As a result of this attack, he almost stopped breathing. We rushed him to the emergency vet, who was able to administer medication. But Rocco's life hung in the balance."

I chomp my thumb as a murmur goes through the crowd. The story has everyone on the edge of their seats.

"Luckily, Rocco's life was saved. He survived the bee attack. This time." Mrs. Bailey dabs at her eyes. The crowd sighs in relief.

"These vicious bees made their nest on the side of our home," she continues.

Beatrix stands up and holds something in the air. From our row, it is hard to get a good look at it.

"We were able to locate it and have the bees removed. But who is to stop these vicious bees from doing the same thing again to all our homes? Who is to stop these bees from attacking another pet? Or worse, a child? As a matter of public safety, I demand that the beehives be removed immediately."

Mrs. Bailey's friends burst into applause. She stands there, soaking it up. For a minute, it reminds me of Beatrix's dance performances and I think Mrs. Bailey might curtsy. She holds up Rocco and makes him wave his little paw. Eventually, she returns to her seat.

Claudia leans toward us. "I didn't get a good look. Could you see the nest they held up?"

We shake our heads.

Mayor Pierce bangs her gavel. "Order, please."

I put my head in my hands. That's it. We've lost. After the cute costumes and that scary story, everyone is on the Baileys' side. Hazel might as well kiss her bees goodbye.

"Meg Garrison," Mayor Pierce calls. "Our next speaker is Meg Garrison."

I gulp.

"Go on," Hazel says. "It's your turn!"

The back of my neck tingles. I feel stuck to my seat.

"Meg Garrison?" the mayor repeats.

Hazel jumps to her feet. "She's here!"

"Mom?" I manage to squeak out.

Mom looks at me steadily. "Your choice, Meg."

My thoughts bounce around. A choice means I could say no. If I wanted to, I could leave this room and never come back.

But that's not who I want to be.

I take Hazel's poster and stand up. My knees seem to be made of jelly. I wobble my way to the lectern. My face is hot like the surface of the sun. I have no idea where to put the poster, so I end up setting it on the floor. It's there if I need it.

I clear my throat.

"My name is Meg Garrison, and I'm here to talk about the bees."

I pause. There's no turning back now.

CHAPTER
34

I look at the crowd, and my mind goes blank.

I can't remember any facts.

I can't remember anything about bees.

In fact, I can't remember anything at all. The contents of my brain are suddenly written in invisible ink.

And I have another problem: I'm dizzy.

Do not faint, I tell myself. *At least not in the next three minutes. After that, you can go ahead and faint if you need to.*

A moment passes and then another. Sweat stripes the back of my neck.

I see the poster at my feet. I could reach down and

grab it. I'd show Hazel's charts and then make my way back to the safety of my seat. But something stops me. I look into the googly eyes of Hazel's cartoon bees, and I remember Ms. Dupart's words. Data doesn't stand alone. Scientists have to make a story. It's up to me. I need to make a story to help them understand. I clear my throat, and then I begin.

"If you asked me about the bees a couple of months ago, I would have been against them. But I've learned a lot since then. And one of the main things I learned is that it's hard to make good decisions when you're afraid."

My face burns. I can feel everyone looking at me, but I keep going.

"The fact is, bees do a lot of good things for people and for our environment. But right now, all around the world, bees are in danger. They need our help."

I tell them about our bee research, surprised to find that I don't need to look at Hazel's poster. I know the facts by heart. We need the bees to pollinate our favorite fruits and vegetables, but it's not just about our food supply. Bees support all kinds of plant and animal life. Our world would be a different place without them.

As I continue to speak, I start to feel even braver. "The letter said that Hazel's bees are breaking laws. It said that bees bother others. But except for what happened with Rocco, the bees haven't bothered anyone."

I glance at Beatrix and Mrs. Bailey.

"I'm really sorry about what happened to Rocco. But, Mrs. Bailey? Can I see the nest you brought in?"

I walk to Mrs. Bailey and hold out my hand. The crowd stirs. Mrs. Bailey looks puzzled but removes the nest from the shopping bag and hands it to me.

The first thing I notice is how lightweight the nest is, almost like paper. It's dull gray, the color of newsprint. The structure reminds me a little of honeycomb. But I see something Beatrix and Mrs. Bailey don't. I have looked inside the honey bees' hive, and that's why I know. This nest isn't yellow and waxy. This would never melt on warm buttered toast.

Before I say what's on my mind, I need to confirm. "This is where the bees came from? Are you sure?"

"I'm positive," Mrs. Bailey says. "Those honey bees are nasty things."

"Honey bees," I say in a whisper. I look at Mrs. Bailey and Beatrix. "So you saw them?"

Mrs. Bailey shudders. "I wish I could forget. They were horrible and mean-looking. Solid black with yellow legs."

"Their bodies were shiny," Beatrix adds. "Evil-looking."

I look at the room. Beatrix and Mrs. Bailey are on one side, and Hazel is on the other. I wait for the teeter-totter feeling but it doesn't come. Teeter-totter moments happen when I'm confused. But I know exactly what to do. I hold the answer in my hands and my time is almost up.

My mouth feels dry. I lean toward the microphone.

"Honey bees aren't black and shiny," I say. "They're fuzzy and striped."

A murmur goes through the crowd. One of the council members, a man with curly hair, pushes forward in his chair. "What is the girl saying?"

I clear my throat and raise my head. "Rocco was attacked by the insects who built this nest. But this nest was not built by honey bees."

"What's that?" asks the curly-haired man again.

"Rocco was not attacked by bees," I say. I take a deep breath. "Rocco was attacked by *wasps*."

The three-minute chime rings.

My time is up.

CHAPTER

35

Immediately, the crowd begins to stir and rumble. The council people cover their microphones and whisper to one another. The whole time, the curly-haired man keeps asking what's happening. Finally, Mayor Pierce bangs her gavel again and again.

"Closed session," she says crisply. "In chambers."

The council members leave through a paneled door.

I walk back to my seat. My dizziness is gone.

"That was amazing," Hazel says.

"Quick thinking," says Mom.

Ms. Dupart's eyes twinkle. "Way to tell a story."

I grin. Mom squeezes my hand.

I turn to Claudia. "The nest was strange. It looked a bit like a honeycomb but felt stiff."

"Probably paper wasps," says Claudia. "Sometimes they become active in early spring, if it's warm enough. Generally, they aren't aggressive this time of year, but maybe little Rocco had some bad luck."

The council members file back into the room.

"I hope it's good news," Hazel says.

Mayor Pierce leans toward the microphone. "We have reviewed tonight's information with interest. First, I would very much like to remind the parties involved that you are neighbors. The first step is always to talk to each other. Try to work things out."

I look at the back of Mrs. Bailey's head and wonder. Maybe things would have been different if Mrs. Bailey talked to Hazel and Astrid before complaining.

"We have reviewed the complaint," continues Mayor Pierce. "We believe there is no statute against the keeping of bees as a home hobbyist. Further, we believe that there was a misidentification as to the species of the attacking insects."

Hazel squeezes my arm.

Mayor Pierce pauses. A smile breaks out across her face. "Further, the council wishes to remind everyone present that y'all happen to live in the great state of North Carolina. This is not the place to live if you don't want to see some insects."

"Amen to that," adds the curly-haired man. Everyone in the room chuckles.

"Therefore, the council has decided that it is *not* in the interest of the town of Willow Pond to have the beehive removed."

Hazel and I gasp. She jumps to her feet.

"Does that mean I get to keep my bees?" she calls out.

Mayor Pierce breaks into a smile. "You get to keep your bees."

Hazel's smile takes up her whole face. She throws her arms high in the air. "Yahoo!"

Our row bursts into cheers. There's scattered applause from around the room. One of the loudest people clapping is grumpy Mr. Shaw. The front rows are very quiet.

"I realize most of our attendance tonight is due to this issue," says Mayor Pierce. "And I also realize it is a school night. So we will pause again for a brief recess. Those who wish to leave may do so."

I look at Mom, who nods. We stand up and file out. Hazel is grinning widely, and I have a smile to match. We did it! Hazel can keep her bees!

When we get to the lobby, Beatrix and Mrs. Bailey are already there, in deep discussion. I see Mom glance at Mrs. Bailey. I can tell Mom wants to go to them, to say hello and smooth things over. She hesitates, like she's trying to decide something. But after a moment, Mom turns back to our group.

"I know it's a bit late," she says. "But I think tonight deserves a celebration. Anyone up for a quick trip to Cooper's for ice cream?"

I beam. "Yes!" I say, and everyone agrees. As we walk down the stone steps, Mom reaches over and squeezes me in a one-armed hug.

"So proud of you, sweetie," she says.

I feel tears in my eyes. I don't know how to say it, but I'm proud of her, too. I may not always understand Mom, and she doesn't always understand me. But I know she's on my side, and tonight, that feels like the most important thing of all.

CHAPTER
36

The next few weeks pass, and I make my way back to the lunchroom. Beatrix, Zoe, and Arshi still sit at our old table. Lucy, one of Beatrix's ballet friends, takes the seat that used to be mine.

Most days, I sit with Hazel and Cora. I can't believe I ever thought Cora was shy. She's actually hilarious and can do perfect impressions of everyone we know. The other day, she pretended she was Coach Pruett shopping at the grocery store, telling all the berries and lettuce they should work harder and be more motivated to achieve their goals. Hazel and I were laughing so hard we cried. Cora says she'll help us put purple streaks in our hair if we want to, but I'm still deciding.

I don't eat lunch with them every day, though. Some-times I sit with Clementine, a red-haired girl who moved here from Asheville and plays the clarinet. Other days, I go to the library for lunch. I know it's kind of funny because I used to hate going there, but being around all those books makes me feel calm. It's the perfect place to go when I need a break.

Hazel's bees are happy. I'm sure there will be lots of honey this summer. Hazel is already talking about giving our neighbors samples, to help everyone see the benefit of bees in the neighborhood. I haven't asked if she's planning to take a sample to the Baileys.

Since it's spring, Mom says it's time for cleaning. One Sat-urday, we all stay home to work. Dad, Conrad, and Elsie are planting in the backyard. Mostly that means that Con-rad tries to stop Elsie from picking all the flowers while Dad works. Mom's upstairs washing windows, and I'm supposed to do the downstairs.

I'm scrubbing at a stubborn spot when I see Beatrix walk by with Rocco. Even after everything, I still feel that pull toward Beatrix when I see her—that feeling of recog-nition. My brain knows we aren't friends anymore, but sometimes my heart forgets.

A few minutes later, Beatrix walks by again.

Then, a few minutes later, she walks by *again*.

So I set down the spray cleaner and paper-towel roll and then step outside.

"Hey," I call.

Beatrix startles, like she is surprised to see me, even though she obviously knows where I live. I walk over to them and scratch Rocco behind his ears. He gets his trademarked blissful droopy-eye expression, and his tongue lolls out of his mouth.

"He always liked you," says Beatrix.

"Yeah," I say, straightening up. "Where's Valentine?"

"Oh," says Beatrix. "That's right—I didn't tell you. She's resting. In a few weeks, she's going to have puppies."

"Wow," I say. It makes me realize how long it's been since we've talked.

Beatrix twists the leash in her hand. "You should come see them after they're born."

I pause for a second, not sure what to say. "I bet they'll be super cute."

"Remember when Rocco was a puppy? He would start to scratch himself and then fall over," Beatrix says.

I smile, remembering. "He was adorable. Still is."

"He was a mess. Still is," says Beatrix, but she's smiling. Rocco seems to know he is being discussed. He sits up straight to show us what a good boy he is.

"I'm glad he's okay after all those stings," I say. "Is your mom still mad about the bees?"

Beatrix shrugs. "She's more mad that I quit ballet."

I stare at her.

"I was really, really tired of it," Beatrix explains. "I

realized I was mostly doing it because everyone expected it. It didn't make me happy anymore."

I know exactly what she means. "So. No more dance?"

Beatrix beams. "I didn't say that. I'm doing contemporary, and I love it. My mom found a teacher who used to live in New York and has all kinds of ideas. She's amazing. Maybe you could come see our performance when we have one."

I let out a big breath. "I don't know. Maybe."

Beatrix frowns, shrugging. "Well, whatever. I'll let you know about my performance, and the puppies, if you want."

I think of everything that happened. Sometimes I do miss her. It would be easy to let everything go back to the way it was.

But there are parts of our friendship I don't want back. I don't want to worry about making her mad.

Dad said that middle school is a moment, but I'm not sure. Sometimes it feels like these three years will last a century. But I want to believe that Beatrix might change. I know I have.

"All right," I say. "Let me know."

Beatrix nods and starts to leave. Then she turns around again.

"Do you ever miss being best friends?"

"Yeah," I say. It's the truth.

Beatrix narrows her eyes. "I still can't believe you chose her over me."

"I didn't choose Hazel over you," I say.

Beatrix shakes her head. "Obviously, you did. She's your new best friend. You picked her. The Bee Girl, of all people."

"Beatrix," I say. "That's not what happened."

But Beatrix doesn't listen. She turns away and heads back down the block, Rocco trotting beside her. I feel a pang as I watch her go. Some things can't be put back together.

Beatrix thinks I picked Hazel over her, but I didn't.

Instead, I picked myself.

CHAPTER 37

The day of our presentation, Dad drops us off at school.

"Bye-bye, busy bees!" Elsie shouts as we get out of the car.

"'Bye, Elsie," Hazel says. "'Bye, tigers!"

Elsie hands Hazel a soggy, half-chewed cereal bar. It's basically a handful of crumbs, held together with spit.

Hazel accepts it happily. "Thank you, Elsie!"

Hazel is kinder than anyone I ever met.

We lug our supplies to Ms. Dupart's room, carefully stacking our boxes against the far wall of the classroom. I double-check that the class set of tablets are charged and ready to go. Our whole presentation depends on it.

My insides flutter the whole day.

"Are you nervous?" I ask Hazel at lunch.

"Nope," Hazel says. "I'm excited to finally have an audience."

That's okay. I'm nervous enough for both of us. My ideas might sound good when we're sitting at Hazel's kitchen table, but in front of an audience, they may not work so well.

We have special permission to leave fifth period fifteen minutes early so we can set up. I place a pair of blindfolds on each table. Hazel passes out the tablets so each student will have one. The laptop is already hooked up to large speakers.

When the bell rings, I want to bolt out the door. But instead, I stand next to Hazel, waiting for everyone to come in.

Ryan picks up a blindfold and swings it in the air like a lasso.

"Are we doing Pin the Tail on the Bee?" he asks. "Or Pin the Tail on My Bee-hind?"

Ms. Dupart talks to him about appropriate classroom behavior.

When everyone sits down, Hazel begins.

"You guys probably already know that I could talk about honey bees all day," Hazel says, grinning. "But Meg and I decided to focus our presentation on life inside the hive. It's time to put on your blindfold. And this will work best if people are silent."

"Beehives aren't really pitch-black," I say. "But they're a lot darker than what we're used to. We want you guys to focus on your other senses."

When everyone is wearing their blindfolds, I give Hazel a thumbs-up.

"Welcome to life inside a beehive," Hazel says.

I press play on the laptop, and the sound of buzzing fills the room. We were lucky enough to find on YouTube a four-hour recording of the sound of buzzing bees. *Oh, what a world we live in,* Dad said when we told him.

The buzzing is extremely realistic. There is a constant background *zzz* sound, but louder and sharper buzzing sounds break through as well. The first time I listened to it blindfolded, it gave me the exact feeling that the bees were crawling right by my head. It looks like other kids feel that way, too, since a few of them reflexively jerk sideways, as if they're trying to avoid a flying bee. Hazel and I grin at each other. So far, so good.

Hazel presses play on another device. "*Plink . . . plink . . . plink.*" When we needed a sound that represented the queen laying an egg, we went to Conrad for help. We recorded him hitting a woodblock, and then we looped the sound to play again and again.

"That sound represents an egg being laid. It only takes a few seconds for a queen to lay an egg. She can lay two thousand eggs in a single day."

All the tablets on the desks begin to vibrate. That buzzing can be heard—*felt*—even above the sounds of the buzzing and plinking. Out of habit, some kids reach for the tablets.

"Don't worry about those. They'll shut themselves off in a few minutes," I say. "Bees use vibration to communicate. They also use chemical signals and dance."

For the last step, we take out large paper fans. Together, we walk up and down the aisles, waving them briskly so everyone can feel the breeze.

"Bees are good at climate control," Hazel says. "The temperature inside is steady, no matter what the weather is like outside. This is how bees survive hot summers and cold winters."

After fanning the class, Hazel and I return to the front. We switch off the sound effects.

"For our next part, you can take off your blindfolds," Hazel says.

"That was super weird but also awesome," one of the eighth graders says.

Ryan shudders. "It was kind of my nightmare."

I smile to myself. I used to be so afraid of the bees, but I'm not anymore.

"For part two, we'll do something different," Hazel says. We walk from table to table, passing out carefully labeled index cards.

"Let's get started," Hazel says. "Who has the drone cards?"

The girls I sat by on the first day of class raise their hands.

"Drones don't do a whole lot," I explain. "Sorry. They're bigger than the worker bees and don't have stingers. Their whole job is to mate with a queen. That's why they have giant eyes—so they can spot any who fly by. But if they mate with her, they die right after."

"That's super depressing," says one of the girls.

Hazel hands them each a pair of oversize novelty sunglasses to represent the drones' enormous eyes.

"All right," I say. "Who got the queen card?"

Ryan stretches his arms above his head and waves them wildly. "Me—I'm the queen! I'm in charge!"

"I used to think that, too," I say. "But the queen isn't really in charge. She lays eggs. And she sends out pheromones, which give messages to the colony."

"Pheromones are kind of complicated," Hazel says. "We couldn't think of a way to represent them all. So we picked one: queen mandibular pheromone. It's basically a signal that tells all the bees that they belong to the queen."

"Well, that *sounds* like I'm in charge," says Ryan.

"Not really," Hazel says. She shakes a bag of lavender pom-poms. "These are pheromones. The queen is going to hand them out. If the queen gives you one, you pass it along to another bee. That's a message that says you belong to the colony. It's important to pass it along so the other bees don't turn on you."

She hands the bag of pom-poms to Ryan. "Use them wisely."

"Oh, I will," he says solemnly.

"Do we have a few larvae and a nursemaid bee?" I ask. Three kids raise their hands.

"All right," Hazel says. "The larvae have recently hatched from their eggs and are being fed by the nursemaid bee. As an egg, your diet was royal jelly, but as a larva, you are fed only honey and pollen. And after you get big enough, you become a nursemaid yourself."

"Worker bees have lots of jobs," I say. "They clean the hive, they build honeycomb, they store pollen, they ripen nectar. But we don't have enough kids in here to do all that, so the other main activity is going to be foraging."

"Raise your hand if you're a forager bee, and Meg will give you a spoon," says Hazel.

I hand out spoons to everyone else, including Ms. Dupart.

"Forager bees leave the hive to look for nectar, which will be turned into honey," Hazel says. "They might fly for miles to find a good source."

"For today, we want you forager bees to look for yellow pom-poms we have hidden around the class," I say. "Even if you find a bunch clustered together, you can only take one to the hive at a time, using your spoon. But if you find another forager bee, you can dance to tell them where the food is located, so they can help you."

"Okay," Hazel says, looking at her watch. "We have ten minutes. Go!"

Our hive begins. The forager bees hunt for nectar. The

nursemaid bee feeds the larvae. Ryan, the queen bee, doesn't pass out his pheromones nicely, like we asked. Instead, he hurls them so they bounce off people's heads. But no one seems to mind.

Hazel and I grin at each other, relieved. We did it.

She turns away to help a foraging bee, and I look at the class. Everyone is moving around, searching for nectar and doing their jobs. They are not quite as busy as real bees, but they aren't bad, for a group of humans. Ms. Dupart is very good at dancing to communicate with the other bees.

I think back to the beginning of the semester, when Hazel told me I could think of a colony as a superorganism. Each bee has their own job—their own part that helps the colony survive.

That feels like a long time ago. Back then, I was afraid of who I would be if I wasn't Beatrix's best friend. I was so concerned about who was in charge and what it all meant. I think I'll always remember that conversation with Hazel. Queen, worker bee, or drone? Who is most important?

Now I know that I wasn't asking the right question.

I don't have to decide if I will be a worker, a queen, or a drone.

I can grow strong. I can work hard. I can fly for miles and always find my way home.

I am a superorganism.

I am everything all at once.

I am my own queen.

ACKNOWLEDGMENTS

Thank you to the courageous, hilarious, and delightful Mary Kate Castellani, the best editor I could ask for.

Huge thanks to my amazing agent Marietta Zacker—who understands me (and this story) so well.

The team at Bloomsbury Children's Books is the bee's knees. Thanks to Cindy Loh, Erica Barmash, Lily Yengle, Phoebe "Porbeagle #1 Fan" Dyer, Beth Eller, Jasmine Miranda, Brittany Mitchell, Courtney Griffin, Jeanette Levy, Donna Mark, Oona Patrick, Stacy Abrams, and Claire Stetzer. It wouldn't have been the same book without you.

Thomas Seeley's *Honeybee Democracy* helped me see bees in an entirely new way. I also spent many happy hours discovering the wondrous details in Piotr Socha's *Bees: A Honeyed History*. Andrew Marani patiently answered questions early on in the process. Sarah Myers showed me her hives and kindly checked my research. Thank you for your help. Any mistakes are my own.

Thanks to every friend I've ever had.

For encouragement and support, thank you to Laura Case, Alice Pierce, Chris Kleinschmidt, Carrie Kavadias, Linda Dupart, Sandy Taylor, and Jared Turner. Thank you to Jackie Skahill, who started as my teacher and became my friend.

Thank you my writer friends, near and far: Camille Andros, Chris Baron, Kirsten Bock, Victoria Coe, Robin Hall, Sarah Hall, J. Kasper Kramer, Mariama Lockington, Michelle Leonard, Cory Leonardo, Larissa Marantz, Stacy McAnulty, Naomi Milliner, Anna Totten, Nicole Pante-leakos, Rebecca Petruck, and Lisa Moore Ramée. Extra big thanks to Rajani LaRocca and Josh Levy for reading, and especially to Caroline Flory for her keen eyes and tender heart.

It would be impossible to write a book about friendship without Gauri Johnston and Aislinn Estes, who have seen me through it all. Love you both.

Writers are borrowers by nature. Thanks to Jon Marino, who inspired Conrad's love of drumming (and Rush); Sarah Moore, who inspired Mom's career; Maggie and Amy Phariss, who helped form Beatrix's interest in dance; Joni Estes, for all the tigers; and Peter Girguis, a (real) marine biologist who studies deep-sea microorganisms. In 2018, Peter's team recorded live footage of the exceedingly rare seven-armed octopus called *Haliphron atlanticus* (only the fourth such sighting ever!). I was so intrigued by this giant pelagic octopus that it became part of Hazel's story. Thanks, friends, for the inspiration.

Finally, thank you to my family. Nora, Leo, and Violet, I'm so lucky to be your mom. Jon, my husband and favorite scientist, I love the way you see the world. Thank you for sharing this life with me.